THE
LEOPARD
Behind the Moon

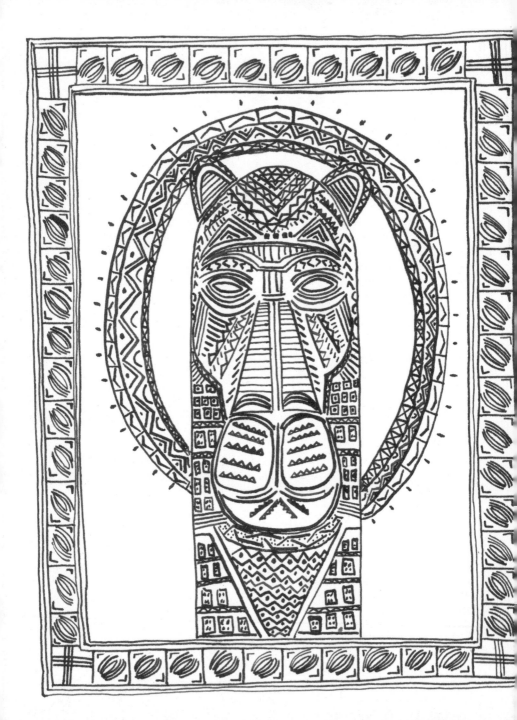

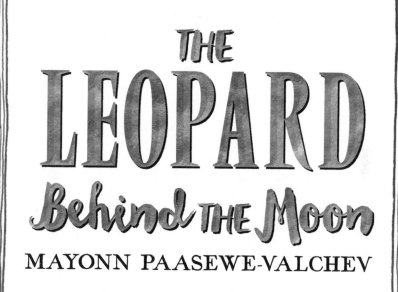

THE LEOPARD
Behind THE Moon

MAYONN PAASEWE-VALCHEV

ILLUSTRATIONS BY
R. Gregory Christie

GREENWILLOW BOOKS
An Imprint of HarperCollinsPublishers

The Leopard Behind the Moon
Text copyright © 2021 by Mayonn Paasewe-Valchev
Illustrations copyright © 2021 by R. Gregory Christie

The text of this book is set in 11-point Plantin.
Book design by Paul Zakris

Library of Congress Cataloging-in-Publication Data

Names: Paasewe-Valchev, Mayonn, author. | Christie, R. Gregory, illustrator.
Title: The leopard behind the moon / by Mayonn Paasewe-Valchev ;
illustrations by R. Gregory Christie.
Description: First edition. |
New York : Greenwillow Books, an Imprint of HarperCollins Publishers, [2021] |
Audience: Ages 8–12. | Audience:
Grades 4–6. | Summary: Ezomo chases after the leopard he believes killed
his father, which leads him and his two friends to open the forbidden
magical door that protects their village.
Identifiers: LCCN 2021025284 (print) | LCCN 2021025285 (ebook) |
ISBN 9780062993618 (hardcover) | ISBN 9780062993632 (ebook)
Subjects: CYAC: Adventure and adventurers—Fiction. | Villages—Fiction. |
Friendship—Fiction. | Leopard—Fiction. | LCGFT: Novels.
Classification: LCC PZ7.1.P17 Le 2021 (print) | LCC PZ7.1.P17 (ebook) |
DDC [Fic]—dc23
LC record available at https://lccn.loc.gov/2021025284
LC ebook record available at https://lccn.loc.gov/2021025285

21 22 23 24 25 PC/LSCH 10 9 8 7 6 5 4 3 2 1
First Edition

GREENWILLOW BOOKS

To All the children of the world.
You are Loved.
♥

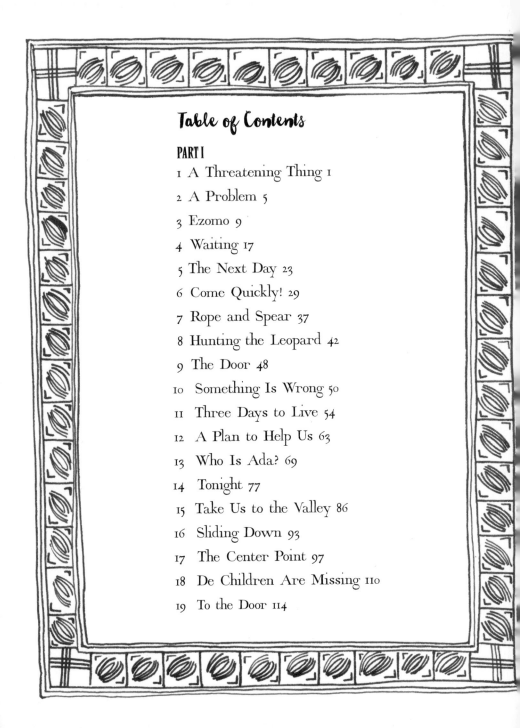

Table of Contents

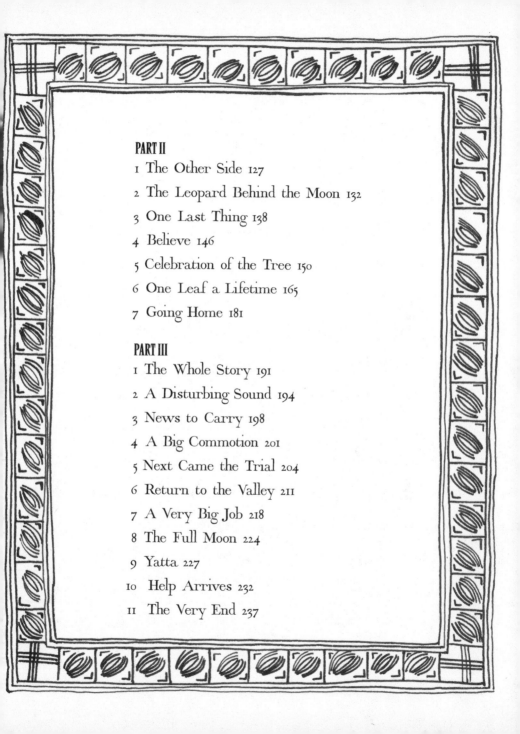

THE LEOPARD

Behind THE Moon

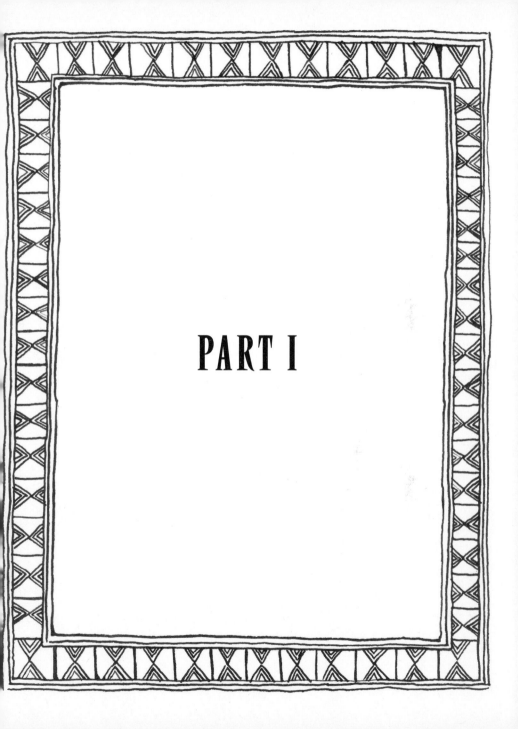

PART I

I

A Threatening Thing

Long before you were born, or perhaps it was long after you had departed, there was a village. This village, which was called Sesa, was burrowed deep in a tropical forest. The village was at the edge of a swamp where sweet thorn trees flourished and formed a hedge no one could pierce. Nestled in the hedge was a rotten door bruised with moss.

Beyond the door stood a dim grove where marula trees, their trunks smothered by climbing plants, crisscrossed over a narrow dirt path carved into the red earth. Twisting and curving, the path eventually led to the heart of the forest. And there the sounds of baboons swinging from trees, wild pigs chasing young impalas, and geckos scurrying across the grass melded with the muffled voices of children playing.

The dirt path continued on and finally stopped at a round plot of dusty red land where years earlier, the villagers had cleared the trees and bushes to construct the largest hut known to mankind: the Palaver Hut. This hut had no walls, and the roof was made from palm branches held up by thick bamboo sticks stationed in the ground. They say the villagers worked five straight days without stopping to eat or sleep to build that hut.

Under the Palaver Hut, women wearing colorful lappas with matching head wraps cooked and quarreled. Some of them dropped chunks of red meat and leafy greens into colossal iron pots. Others stirred rice with long wooden spoons. A few of the women sat on wicker benches and peeled yams. Some pounded cassavas in mortars.

Surrounding the Palaver Hut were tall fever trees with sprawling branches that cast a shadow over the young children playing hide-and-seek and the chickens searching for beetles and locusts to eat. On these towering fever trees, the talking kingfisher birds perched and listened to the women, their eardrums sharpened for news to carry afar. On this day, it was Muna who was leading the quarrel.

"First, we shall quarrel about the sleeping sun!" Muna

bellowed and dropped three pieces of fleshy meat into a boiling pot of water. Muna was the tallest woman in Sesa, and whenever she spoke, the other women had to stand on their toes and stretch their necks to see her face.

"Yesterday," Muna continued, "the sun slept so much we had to rely on the fireflies for light during the day."

"De sun is getting lazy-o!" shouted Chima from atop a bucket. Chima was the fussiest woman in Sesa, and so short that whenever she spoke, the other women had to bend their necks to see her face. She was also a terrible cook, and so she was the only woman in Sesa who wasn't allowed to boil a single grain of rice or toss a single piece of meat into any pot under the Palaver Hut. Embarrassed that she couldn't cook, Chima spent most of her days tormenting others by starting frivolous quarrels and then challenging her victims to a wrestling match to settle the argument.

"If we don't do something about de sun's laziness," Chima continued, "we will be forced to live in darkness!"

Grumbling and loud chatter filled the hut as the women talked among themselves and agreed that something had to be done soon about the sun's laziness.

"Do not worry," Muna said while flapping her hands to

settle the crowd. "I promise to go see the Elders tomorrow and lodge a complaint against the sun."

Managing to pacify the others with her promise, Muna went on: "After we finish talking about the sun, we will quarrel about our declining crops."

The women nodded and murmured.

"And when we finish talking about the sun and the crops," Muna continued, "we will quarrel about something threatening our very existence."

A gasp escaped from somewhere in the crowd. Several women frowned. Others placed hands on their hips and tapped their feet. A few women twisted their mouths and rolled their eyes.

Muna took a deep breath and lowered her voice. "We shall decide what to do about Ezomo."

2

A Problem

Behind the Palaver Hut was a wide mud road that led to the main village compound. The villagers had named this main compound Passtru because it was built in the center of the town, and people had to pass through it to reach the rest of the village. The wide mud road, after passing through Passtru, led to the river, where each day the men of Sesa gathered on canoes made from hollowed tree trunks and rowed to the other side to discuss important affairs. Once on the far riverbank, they sat in rows under the palm trees and looked out over the village farm.

The front row was occupied by men with bald heads and gray beards wearing white robes: the Elders. They were the great-grandchildren of the men and women who had discovered Sesa long ago, so they held the highest rank in the village. They sat on wooden stools, while the other men sat on the red earth. Seated behind the Elders were hunters, fishers, and farmers holding spears, shovels, and whatever else they could bring to show their status. The load carriers, wood-carvers, and basket makers sat in the third row with small pride in their eyes since they didn't have to sit in the last row, which was reserved for men who, according to the Elders, lacked the talent and skill to contribute fully to the village.

On this day, Sao, the village's orator, was leading the meeting. He stood before the crowd and glanced at his palm. Written there in red dye was a single word—*Ezomo*.

"Men of Sesa!" Sao shouted. "This meeting is important-o."

"E-hey!" the other men replied in unison.

"But before we talk, we must prepare our bellies, which if left hungry, will not support our throats when time comes to speak."

"E-hey!" the other men shouted, at which point Toba stood and dashed to a canoe to perform one of the few duties he was permitted to do since he had stopped speaking. No one knew what had caused Toba to stop speaking. One morning while standing in the doorway of his hut, he'd attempted to greet his neighbors, but sound refused to leave his mouth. Some suspected witchcraft, some claimed a jealous spirit had stolen his voice, and some said his voice was merely resting.

The villagers had burdened their mouths for weeks with speculation about Toba's predicament, so their tongues were content to watch in silence the day the Elders ordered Toba and his family to leave Passtru and go to Noroad.

Noroad was the compound reserved for men and women with no talent or skill. The Elders had named it "Noroad" because it was on the outskirts of Sesa, and there was no road leading to it or from it. In Noroad, there were no mud huts, only flimsy shacks made from twigs and palm leaves. "If you can't contribute fully, you have no business in a real hut," the Elders had said to Toba.

Before Toba lost his voice, he was a prominent hunter and had led many hunting adventures across the vast forest, venturing to places no other hunter dared to go. But the Elders had proclaimed that without words to give orders or words to teach others, Toba was of little use to the village.

Today, Toba returned from the canoe with a large pot, and inside of it was rice drizzled with palm oil and pieces of smoked fish. The pot was passed around for each man to grab a handful until the last grain was gone, at which time Sao licked palm oil from all ten of his fingers, wiped his mouth with the back of his hand, and began to speak.

"Men of Sesa! We have gathered here to discuss a problem that must be dealt with sooner rather than later." Sao glanced once more at the writing on his palm and shook his head. "Men of Sesa. Ezomo continues to test our patience."

"E-hey!"

"He continues to threaten our existence!"

"E-hey!"

"For years we've swallowed his ways even though it pained our throats."

"E-hey!"

"But when an eel refuses to ease out of its larva, one must extract the meat with bare hands."

"E-hey!"

Sao lowered his voice. "Men of Sesa. It is time we take action against Ezomo."

3

Ezomo

While the men gathered by the riverbank to eat and confer, and the women gathered under the Palaver Hut to cook and quarrel, the children gathered on the village farm to learn how to be good citizens of Sesa.

The farm was divided into three sections. The smallest section was a grassy plot where goats and sheep grazed on yellow-green grass. The middle section was divided into grids, and on each grid grew potato greens, yams, cassava, or maize. The largest section of the farm was dry and dusty, and peppered with weeds. Encircling it all were mango trees, where yellow and red fruit huddled under green leaves and produced a sweet smell that brushed over the entire farm. Under one of these mango trees was where the children sat in rows and listened to lectures from a grandmother with no teeth who they called Oma.

Oma taught the children how to plant crops, how to milk goats, how to groom themselves properly, and how to be good helpers to their mothers and fathers.

"Ama!" Oma yelled.

A plump girl wearing a yellow lappa sprang to her feet, bowed, and sat back down.

"Togar!" Oma yelled.

A boy wearing a purple-and-orange wrapper stood up, bowed, and sat down. Oma carried on this way until she'd finished calling the names of all the children sitting in the front row, those with bloodlines to the Elders. Next, she called the names of children sitting in the middle rows. These were the children of hunters, fishers, and farmers, and after they stood and bowed, Oma called the names of children sitting near the back, those whose parents were load carriers, wood-carvers, and basket makers. Sitting behind those children, in the very last row, were the children of parents with no talent or skill. That was where Ezomo's two friends, Chimama and Muja, sat, and they too stood and bowed when Oma shouted their names.

"Ezomo!" was the last name to be called, and once it fled Oma's mouth, her eyes traveled over the heads of all the other children to the limb of the mango tree where Ezomo sat alone. He was gazing across the river and paid her no attention.

"Ezomo!" Oma shouted once more above the snickering of the other children, who had all turned their necks to gape at Ezomo. Again, her voice traveled in vain.

Oma marched to the tree trunk and whacked Ezomo's leg. "Ezomo!"

Ezomo flinched and looked down. Oma wore a brown lappa wrapped tightly around her gaunt body—like a moth in a cocoon. In her right hand, she held a chewing stick which she regularly fed to her mouth to be gnawed by her gums.

She wagged her chewing stick at Ezomo. "You here today?"

Ezomo scratched his head. "Huh?"

"Stand urp!"

Ezomo leapt to the ground. He looked to his left and right as if seeing the farm for the first time. Then his attention settled on the faces watching him and he felt ashamed. His shame was so great that after it consumed him, it crept to some of the other children, and Ezomo saw it staring back at him through their eyes. He looked down and fidgeted with the dingy blue wrapper around his waist. He wished for darkness to descend and suffocate the morning light so that no one, not even the grasshoppers and beetles crawling in the grass, could see his face.

"Bow!" Oma snapped, scattering his thoughts.

Ezomo arched his back and lowered his head. A boom of laughter erupted from the other children. He raised his eyes and saw tongues quaking with joy.

"Your wrapper is gone!" Togar said, pointing to Ezomo's tattered wrapper, which was bunched up between his thighs.

"And so is your hair!" Muja shouted back at Togar.

The laughter continued, but this time everyone turned their attention away from Ezomo's wrapper to Togar's thinning hairline.

"Fix yurr wrapper!" Oma rebuked. "Useless boy!" She shook her head and ambled back to her spot to begin the morning lesson.

"We will begin by discussing Ada," Oma said. "Who remembers hur?"

A skinny boy sitting in the front row wagged his hand, and Oma nodded her approval for him to speak.

"Ada was the girl who opened the village door," the boy, whose name was Ebo, said.

"Uh-huh. What else did Ada do?"

"She went out alone at night."

Oma extracted her chewing stick from her mouth and wagged it at Ebo, splashing spit on those in the front row. "Are children allowed out alone at night?"

"No Oma," Ebo responded.

"And what happened when Ada went out alone at night and opened the durr?"

"Something bad happened," said Ebo.

Oma yanked her earlobe. "Did you children hear that?" she yelled, startling them. "Something evil happened when Ada opened the durr!"

Whispers and murmuring and fear filled the spaces between the children.

Oma took a deep breath and exhaled. "Was Ada punished for opening the durr?"

"Yes. She was sent to the Valley," Ebo said.

"Uh-huh. Is the Valley a nice place for children?"

Ebo shook his head. "No. It's dark and cold. Bats live there."

"And when will Ada leave the Valley?" Oma asked, pacing back and forth and stirring up the dust.

"Never. She will die there."

"Correct!" Oma narrowed her eyes. "If you ever see the durr in the forest, will you open it?"

"No Oma!" the children yelled in unison. Except for Ezomo. He was busy drawing circles in the soil with his finger.

"Our ancestors built the durr to protect us, and we must keep it shrut!" Oma continued. "If you ever see the durr in the forest, hide yurr face and run away."

Chimama raised her hand.

"What you want?" Oma said, pointing her chewing stick at Chimama.

"What evil thing happened when Ada opened the door eh?" Chimama asked.

Oma placed one hand on her hip and glared at Chimama. "Why yurr mother can't cook eh? Save yurr stupid questions for Chima," Oma said and spat brown phlegm on the ground. She then pointed her stick to Togar, who had his hand raised, leaving Chimama and the rest of the children to once again imagine what was really behind the village door and what evil thing had happened when Ada opened it. And imagine they did.

For as far back as the villagers of Sesa could recall, the door had always been there, in the forest, and since no one knew why it was there—and only a few people had ever actually seen it—they'd invented many stories about it. Some said all the young animals died the night Ada opened the door. Others said the crops stopped growing for an entire year. Evil spirits lived on the other side, ready to bite your hands off. Behind the door was where crocodiles waited for children to swallow.

After Oma finished answering Togar's question, and around the time she began teaching the children how to mend huts, Ezomo left. Not physically, but mentally. He was imagining being invisible and strolling past Oma and down to the farm to hide between the maize plants, and had it not been for a fat mosquito landing on his eyelid and disturbing his thoughts, Ezomo would have remained in his daydreams.

He rubbed his eyelid and stretched his neck to see above

the heads of the other children, who were watching Oma demonstrate how to tie a three-way knot with two palm leaves. Ezomo pressed his hands into the red earth and eased himself down. Lying flat on his back, he listened to Oma's gummy, toothless voice.

"Learning under this tree is yurr first duty," he heard her say. Those were the same words the Elders had uttered to him many times. Once children in Sesa turned four, they were required to spend six days a week learning their lessons under the mango tree.

"Even if you're sick, we must see you under the mango tree," the Elders had told him.

Ezomo waited for Oma's shuffling feet to settle. Then he turned onto his belly, held his breath, and slithered behind the mango tree. He wriggled farther into the leafy shadows and hoped Oma wouldn't spot him. Ezomo needed to get to a place he considered far more important than the mango tree.

4
Waiting

Behind the mango tree was an abandoned fruit stand and a grassy footpath. Ezomo crawled down the footpath, between wild ferns and thistle weeds, and kept crawling until the path matured into a narrow road with yellow hibiscus plants growing along the shoulder. He stood and brushed dirt from his bare chest and legs.

The day was young, and with the sun asleep, gray clouds played jubilantly in the sky and cast a gloomy veil over Sesa. Ezomo inhaled the morning air and released it through his mouth. The tightness in his stomach softened. He felt small peace.

Eventually, the narrow road joined the wide mud road, and together, they carried Ezomo to Passtru. With everyone attending to various morning duties, the compound and all its commodities—pots, pans, mortars—were left to rest, and the only sound lingering was from an old goat munching on a cassava peel. Ezomo scuttled through Passtru, stopping briefly by a basket of corn to tuck one in his wrapper. Then he slipped behind a mud hut where tall elephant grass swallowed his body and spared his head.

Ezomo shuffled between the blades of grass, swatting frisky katydids and restless mosquitos. In the distance, the forest with its baboons, impalas, and geckos awaited him. Ezomo walked and swatted until he'd passed the shadow of the Palaver Hut and reached the lip of the forest where there was a large rock upon which he sat most days to pass the time.

Ezomo had come to know that rock three years earlier when his father died. The week his father passed, Ezomo's mother, Yatta, had tried explaining the idea of death to Ezomo but spoke so indirectly—in parables and proverbs—that Ezomo thought dying was a temporary mishap and kept waiting for his father to return from a hunting contest the Elders had arranged. Every morning at sunrise, Ezomo had trekked to the forest to wait for his father. And every day at sunset, he'd returned home disappointed and confused that his father had never showed.

One day while Ezomo sat restlessly under the mango tree not listening to Oma, he overheard Chimama and Muja whispering about the leopard that had killed his father. When Ezomo asked Chimama and Muja what they were discussing, they pretended not to hear him and brushed him off.

Another morning, while Ezomo waited on the rock for his father, one of the village's many talking birds, Bisa, had been perched on a tree nearby. Bisa watched Ezomo for a while and decided he would put some sense into the poor boy's head.

"Ezomo!" Bisa called from atop the tree. "Why e come here every day?"

"Waiting for my Papa," Ezomo said.

"E no come back Ezomo."

"Why not?"

"Because e killed by leopard. Go home."

Ezomo ran home and repeated Bisa's words to his mother.

"Bisa is cantankerous. A sour bird he is!" Yatta sputtered. Then speaking plainly, without proverbs, Yatta confirmed that Bisa—cantankerous and all—was telling the truth. When Yatta finished speaking, Ezomo felt a heavy lump settle in his throat and block his voice, so that his eyes were forced to translate his words into tears. And yet still, Ezomo kept returning to the rock every morning.

After a year, the lump abandoned Ezomo's throat and settled in his muscles, making them tense with anger. So much so that one morning, Ezomo marched to the compound where the Elders lived and, finding them sitting on a veranda drinking palm juice, he spoke with rage vibrating on his tongue and asked them why they let his father die. With their bellies full of palm juice, they'd laughed at him and told him to put aside his grief and start contributing to Sesa like everyone else. Then they ordered him to go home.

On the way there, Ezomo felt the lump leave his muscles and rest on his heart. Over the years, the lump grew big and powerful and swallowed Ezomo's feelings. And one day, the lump got tired and departed, taking with it parts of Ezomo and leaving behind only a shadow of the boy he once was. It was around that time that the villagers grew impatient with Ezomo. They complained that because he wasn't learning anything, he wasn't helping to carry the village forward. Sesa was self-sustaining. If the village was to continue existing, the knowledge of the old had to be passed down to the young, and every villager, no matter what their age, needed to contribute. Ezomo, they said, contributed nothing but stale grief. He was setting a bad example for the other children and threatening the existence of all of them.

Today, after idling on the rock for some hours, Ezomo finally left the forest. He walked back the way he had come, back between tall elephant grass, back behind the mud hut, then along the outskirts of the main village compound to meet the gravel path leading to his living quarters.

Strolling on the same path were Chimama and Muja returning from the farm. Wherever Muja was, Chimama was usually nearby. They were together so much that the villagers said they had been brother and sister in a former life.

"Want to eat with us?" Chimama said, holding out her hand to show Ezomo a ripe mango. "We stole it," she said and twirled her tongue around. Her tongue was too big for her mouth, and it was restless too, so it congregated with her teeth, played with her bottom lip, and twirled around her jaws. It also sometimes made saying words with *s* and *z* difficult for Chimama, especially when she was nervous.

Ezomo, Chimama, and Muja sat in a ditch alongside the road and took turns eating the fruit. Ezomo sucked the seed and licked yellow juice from his wrist as he listened to Chimama tell a story Oma had shared earlier that day about a clever spider who tricked a king and stole his crown. Then he listened to Muja talk about the boys who sat in the front row and which ones he wanted to beat up and for what reason.

Maybe it was the sweetness of the mango, or the light in Chimama's eyes as she retold Oma's story, or Muja's foolish gestures that illustrated his macho promises, for as Ezomo listened, something shifted inside him. He felt movement in his heart, like feathers sweeping, and for the first time since he'd learned about his father's death, Ezomo cracked a small smile. He wasn't expecting it, hadn't anticipated it—it surprised him.

Unbeknownst to Ezomo, his heart had been working for years to pry itself open, to squeeze weak light through stubborn cracks. But it was all a wasted effort—because a terrible thing was about to happen, and that terrible thing would cause Ezomo's heart to suffer greatly and seal up once more.

5
The Next Day

The next day was rainy and gloomy. It was also rest day: the one day the villagers didn't do arduous work. On rest day, the villagers held picnics on the riverbank, danced to the drums in the market square, or lounged under palm trees near their various living quarters. But on this rest day, Sesa was unusually quiet. It was as if the people suspected something terrible was about to happen, and they were waiting in their huts for the looming evil to pass with the rain.

In the compound where the load carriers, wood-carvers, and basket makers lived was a mud hut that tilted to one side and appeared to be on the brink of falling over. Inside that hut, Ezomo and Yatta sat on the bare earth eating boiled cassava while listening to water drop into the buckets planted around the room to catch rain falling from the leaky roof.

"You think the sun will shine today?" Ezomo asked his mother.

Yatta sucked her teeth: "Steoooeow." She had two ways of sucking her teeth, and each had a particular meaning. When she protruded her lips and sucked her teeth, it sounded like "steew" and meant somebody had said or done something foolish. And when she sucked her teeth from the side of her jaw, it sounded like "steoooeow" and meant she was annoyed or vexed.

"The sun is like a lion without teeth—useless!" Yatta said.

Ezomo turned his face away from his mother and eyed a worm wriggling into the earth.

"Why you worry about the sun?" Yatta asked.

He shrugged and continued observing the worm.

"Ezomo . . ." Yatta reached across the pan of cassava and grabbed his hand. "You can't spend your whole life sitting on a rock. A bird who refuses to fly will eat worms all its days and forfeit the tasty insects in the sky."

Ezomo yanked his hand away and, with his forefinger, he drew a circle around the worm.

Yatta brushed her palm over her face and took a deep breath. "The people are talking, Ezomo. They say you spend too much time sitting on that rock in the forest and no time learning under the mango tree. They say you are becoming useless—like the sun."

Ezomo didn't look up. He pulled the worm out of the earth and watched it squirm around the grooves of his palm.

Yatta tapped his leg. "Ezomo?"

"They don't want me under the mango tree," Ezomo said and dropped the worm.

"Who don't want you under the tree?"

"Oma—and the other children too."

"Why you say this?"

He glanced at his mother, then quickly looked down.

"Oma makes me sit alone. And—"

"And what?"

"When the others make fun of me, her eyes smile."

Yatta didn't respond. She sat for a while watching Ezomo torment the worm. Then she looked around their hut. It was tiny, with just enough space for the two of them and the few items they owned. In the corner were two rattan baskets she hoped to sell. Before the aches in her arms and chest arrived, she used to weave as many as ten baskets a week. Now her body allowed her only two a week. Lying in the dirt next to the baskets was a cooking pot holding the two cassava roots she had salvaged for their evening meal. An ear of corn Ezomo had given her rested in a bowl beside the pot. In another corner was a warped wooden bench and on top of it sat a bucket with a dirty rag hanging over the rim. Underneath the bench was an oil lamp and a rumpled blanket. In the third corner was a wheelbarrow partially covered with dust and a black head wrap.

Yatta rested her eyes on a crack in the wall where the gloominess of the day seeped through. Underneath her breath, she began counting the holes in the sides and roof of the hut. There were twenty-two.

"Ezomo," she said with a trembling voice, "you mustn't look at Oma's eyes. Look at her mouth and hands, so you can learn to mend our hut. Let Oma teach you how to fix your father's wheelbarrow, so you can tote the loads of the farmers and fishers."

Ezomo offered his mother a blank stare.

"I don't know how long the Elders will let us stay here without us contributing fully," Yatta continued. "We have your father's debts to pay. I weave baskets till my knuckles bleed. . . ." She flipped her palms and showed Ezomo her scabbed knuckles. "And still we eat dry cassava and sleep on dirt. They have threatened to send us to Noroad."

Ezomo turned his cheek to his mother and avoided her eyes.

"You must stop behaving like the sun," Yatta said, wringing her hands. "In two years, you will pass from childhood to manhood. Are you prepared? Your grief is the only place you've shown that you are strong. I've given you every root in the forest to loosen your sadness, and still, you hold on to it. What more must I do Ezomo?"

Ezomo pressed his palms against his ears and looked up.

"Ezomo!" Yatta yelled and clutched her chest.

Ezomo uncovered his ears and looked in his mother's eyes to see sorrow fighting anger. "Mamie . . . maybe Papa—"

"If you don't help me," Yatta pleaded, "I don't know what will happen to us."

Ezomo looked solemnly at the ground and watched

the worm disappear under the soil. "Please, Ezomo, I beg you—rest your grief and help me." Yatta buried her face in her lappa and sobbed. Had she looked up, she would have seen Ezomo easing himself off the dirt and walking out of the hut.

6

Come Quickly!

Outside, the rain was in no hurry to join the earth, so it fell slowly, in light drops, then swirled with dirt to form mud puddles to be trampled by children. Ezomo leapt over a puddle in front of his hut and scurried across the compound and down the gravel path. He looked back to make sure Yatta wasn't trailing him and saw only their run-down living quarters blurred by rain. His mother's words were scattered in his head. Her sobs echoed in his ears.

"What can a useless boy like me do?" Ezomo thought and hung his head low. The image of his mother's scabbed knuckles flickered across his mind. He examined the dark knuckles on his fingers—they were smooth and without cuts. He picked up a small stone and tapped its curvy and sharp edges. He rubbed the stone briskly against his hand until the skin felt raw and he spotted a fleck of blood budding on his forefinger. Uncurling his palm, Ezomo released the stone and continued walking.

About a quarter of a mile down the road, he abandoned the path and leapt into the mimosa bushes. He stopped to observe a tree frog with bright red eyes resting on a wet leaf. He cupped his hands around the leaf and slid the frog into his grip. Then he scrambled back onto the road.

As Ezomo walked, he blew warm air into his cupped hands and peeked with one eye at the frog hopping around his palms. He thought of a story Oma once told about a brave frog that rescued a colony of tadpoles from the beak of an eagle. "You're not brave at all," Ezomo whispered to the frightened frog. "You're like me."

He set the frog free and pulled two leaflets from a palm tree. Placing one leaf on top of the other, he attempted to tie a three-way knot, but all he managed to make was a mess. Ezomo flung the battered fronds into the bushes and bowed his head.

As Ezomo walked on, he sang a song. It was a song his father had sung when he took Ezomo to cart cassava and yams from the farm to the village market, or when they waited by the riverbank for the fishermen to return with nets full of eels needing toting. The memories of his father had faded, but the song was still sharp in his mouth. It was about a baby bird whose wings were stolen.

Who stole your wings small bird?
Who stole your pride?
Get up and try, get up and fly.
Dry the shame from your eyes small bird.
Get up and try, get up and fly.

Ezomo finally reached the main village compound and choosing on this day to spare himself the trek through the wet elephant grass, he cut between a row of houses to join the wide mud road, reaching soon the round plot where the Palaver Hut stood empty.

He maneuvered between the fever trees, trampling weeping ferns and bush honeysuckles, until he stood before his rock. The sun had still not woken up to embrace the morning, so a coolness roamed the air and settled in the grove. Ezomo climbed onto the rock. He shuddered and crossed his arms over his bare chest. He sat that way for a while, staring at the leafy canopy of trees, listening to the crinkling sound of wet branches settling.

When the morning had long passed and taken with it the rain, Ezomo shifted his attention to the small insects crawling across the soil. He jumped off his rock, knelt, and cupped his hands around a dung beetle. He spread his palms apart and watched the insect crawl over his skin and disappear into the grass. He drew pictures in the soil with his finger. First, he drew the face of a boy with a tear falling from his eye. Then he smoothed the soil and drew a picture of a river surrounded by palm trees. When he finished drawing, he lay flat on the rock and gazed at the sky—his thoughts darting around with no aim.

It was then that Ezomo heard something rustling in the trees. At first, he disregarded it but then he heard a noise he'd never heard before—a raspy yowl. He sat up and held his breath. His eardrums waited for sound. Lingering raindrops dripped on leaves. A bird cawed somewhere in the distance. Ezomo exhaled and eased back down on the rock.

Seconds later, he heard the raspy yowling again, louder

and clearer. He bolted upright. The hairs on his arms stood with him as he peered around.

"Mamie . . . ," he called to the silence.

Silence said nothing.

"Muja . . ." He stood still and listened. "Chimama . . ."

He abandoned his rock and crept into the dense vegetation, parting soggy branches and stepping over the leafy vines clinging to his legs. A lone mongoose scurried by, and Ezomo watched it disappear into tall, feathery grass. He ducked under a creeper plant and edged deeper into the woodland. Then his feet came to an abrupt stop, and his eyes widened when they saw what was behind a curtain of damp leaves. It had its head bowed in a pit and was licking the water resting there, claws pressed into red mud. Ezomo covered his mouth with his palm.

Ezomo saw sharp green eyes blink and thick fur shift and settle. Then the leopard lifted its head and yawned, showing off big yellow fangs. Ezomo felt like a tree rooted to the ground and if the leopard had charged at him, he would not have been able to move. It was only when the animal bowed its head again and resumed drinking that Ezomo convinced his feet to back away, one careful step at a time until he was once more beside his rock.

"Papa . . . ," Ezomo whispered. Then he bolted out of the grove, through the bushes, past the Palaver Hut, and down the wide mud road toward Passtru.

In Passtru, the children were playing soccer while their mothers sat around braiding each other's hair. Ezomo raced past them and made his way to a banana tree where three hunters sat eating yam and fish from a large bowl. Two more hunters were curled up on rattan mats sleeping away the day. Ezomo stood before them shaking and panting and announced that he'd seen the leopard that had killed his father and that they needed to come quickly and capture it.

One of the hunters yawned, and the other two continued eating without glancing at Ezomo. "Useless boy," one murmured with a mouth full of yam. "It's rest day."

Ezomo frowned and repeated his news with a trembling voice, but the hunters continued eating. If Ezomo was speaking the truth and not imagining things, the leopard, they reasoned, would be there tomorrow.

"Go keep the leopard company until we come. You got

nothing better to do anyway," the hunter with a giant gap between his teeth muttered.

The other hunters laughed.

Ezomo's face felt hot. The excitement in his belly crumbled and scattered. He felt ashamed for believing that anyone would listen to him. How foolish to think the hunters would follow him to the forest to capture the leopard. He was just a useless boy. With slumped shoulders, he walked away.

Ezomo headed toward the river, tears oozing down his cheeks. The image of the leopard drinking water flashed in his mind and woke up a memory of him and his father eating roasted corn by the river. But the memory, having been summoned many times before, was tired and quickly retreated to rest.

A group of girls returning from the river with buckets of water on their heads passed by. "Useless boy," one of them whispered. Their laughter clinked and clanked in the air.

Ezomo bowed his head and invited a memory from yesterday—the one of Chimama, Muja, and him sitting alongside the road eating a mango. Each time Chimama had laughed, her eyes sparkled, and when he searched behind their shine, he'd found no hidden motives.

Ezomo took a deep breath and wiped his eyes with the back of his hand. Then, picking up his pace, he turned away from the river and toward the market.

7

Rope and Spear

In the market a few vendors were sweeping trash from their stalls. A small crowd gathered near the back. The scent of ripe fruit hung in the air and enticed the flies buzzing around. Ezomo stepped over a half-eaten mango and wandered to Old Man Flomo's stall.

Old Man Flomo sold fried eels wrapped in banana leaves and told stories. Because his tales were good, and his eels tasty, there was usually a crowd hanging around his stall, even on rest days.

When Ezomo arrived, Old Man Flomo was telling a story about a greedy monkey. Whenever Ezomo listened to Flomo's tales, he listened with a desperate ache to hear stories of boys and girls like him, but like all the tales told in

Sesa, Flomo's stories were always about brave and clever characters who showed great strength in tragedy and overcame adversity quickly. They didn't have mothers with scabbed knuckles or useless boys with sadness that wouldn't loosen in them.

Standing on his toes, Ezomo scanned the crowd for Chimama and Muja.

"You all right today, Ezomo?" Flomo called out to him.

"Have you seen—"

"*Shhh . . . ,*" said Ido, a stocky boy with a big scar on his cheek who had been completely immersed in the story before Ezomo showed up and interrupted it.

Two familiar faces turned toward Ezomo.

"Hey," Chimama whispered, squeezing her way through the crowd to stand beside him. Muja followed behind her.

"Wetin you crying about?" Chimama whispered in Ezomo's ear.

Ezomo shrugged.

"Tell me," Chimama said, lifting Ezomo's chin.

"I . . . I . . . I saw—"

"You saw what?" Muja said, leaning into Ezomo.

"I saw the leopard that killed my Papa."

Muja gasped. "What?"

Ido turned around. *"Shhh!"*

Chimama grabbed Ezomo's hand and pulled him behind an empty yam stall. "What leopard you talking 'bout eh?"

When Ezomo told Chimama and Muja about the leopard in the forest and explained that the hunters had refused to go and capture it, Muja drummed his chest and proclaimed that if anyone was going to capture the leopard, it would be him.

"My father prepared me well-o," Muja said with a hand on his heart.

It was true. Before his father Toba lost his speech, he had taken Muja hunting most afternoons and taught him how to catch rabbits and wild birds.

"What it look like eh?" Chimama asked as the three friends hurried out of the market.

Ezomo stretched his arms far apart. "This big. Like a baobab tree."

Chimama's mouth opened. "Eh! A big one-o."

"Yes, very big. And eyes green like a grasshopper," Ezomo said.

Muja raised his chin. "I've killed a beast like that before."

"When?" Chimama asked.

"Long time ago. With my father in the forest."

"You'll need a thpear," Chimama said.

"A what?" asked Muja.

"A thpear!" Chimama pantomimed the throwing of a spear into the bushes.

"Oh, a spear. Yes!"

"And a rope too," Ezomo added.

"Yes, to tie him up like this," Muja said while moving his finger in a circular motion like a tornado. "Actually, a net might be better. . . ." Muja rubbed his chin. "So we can trap him. Let's stop by Noroad on our way. Got to grab my father's hunting bag."

"What Toba got in the bag eh?" Chimama asked.

Ezomo glanced at the sky while Muja named the many tools in Toba's hunting bag. He saw dark clouds drifting. He looked around. The leaves on the trees rustled. Branches swayed. "A storm is coming. We must hurry," he said.

"You know how to hunt in rain?" Chimama asked Muja.

"I can hunt in rain, drought, famine, and whatever the earth brings me," Muja said and pounded his chest with closed fists.

Chimama rolled her eyes and laughed. "By the time we reach Noroad, rain will be falling. Better we get thpear and net from main compound eh?"

Muja slapped Chimama's arm. "You thinking good today-o. Yes, let's get the spear and net from the main compound."

In the bushes, the beetles and katydids listened to the friends cement their plans and hurry off, and like the other insects in the grass, they began searching for a place to hide from the storm.

8

Hunting the Leopard

The friends managed to seize a rusty spear from a pile of broken tools left behind a hut. They snatched a torn fishing net from the veranda of one of the fishermen.

"This net big enough to trap him," Muja said assuredly.

The kingfisher birds perched in the fever trees eyeballed the children as they scuttled out of the main compound toward the forest.

"We better get Toba eh?" Chimama said to Muja. She clenched her fist around a stone she'd found on the path.

Muja ignored her and marched ahead with the spear raised as if he expected the leopard to appear at any moment. The net dangled over his left arm.

Ezomo kept quiet. He was imagining running home to

tell his mother he had captured the leopard. An image of him and Yatta toting the leopard in his father's wheelbarrow flashed through his mind. He conjured up a memory of his father and placed it alongside the road to wave at them as they passed by with the leopard. Then his father joined them, and together they pushed the beast through the entire village.

"Where e going?"

It was Bisa, that cantankerous bird, interrupting Ezomo's thoughts. He had been following the children and wanted to know why they were in such a hurry.

"Going to catch a leopard," announced Muja.

"A-hey!" Bisa landed near the children's feet. "What leopard?"

Chimama pointed to Ezomo. "The one that killed his father."

Bisa covered his eyes with his wing and shook his head.

"Don't cover your eyes-o," Muja said. "You will need them to see the beast I'm about to capture."

Bisa fell on his back and burst into laughter. "Go home! There's no leopard."

"I saw it!" said Ezomo.

"No e didn't."

"I swear! I—"

"E didn't!"

"I did!"

Bisa sighed. "Maybe e were dreaming?"

Ezomo stroked his chin and gave small thought to Bisa's question. Was it possible he had dreamt the leopard? But those sharp fangs were real. And he'd seen green eyes blink and heard a soppy sound each time the leopard licked the water.

"No. It wasn't a dream," Ezomo said sharply, turning away from Bisa.

"Good luck finding something not there," Bisa screeched as the children disappeared under an umbrella of drooping branches.

Ezomo, Muja, and Chimama hadn't been in the forest long when the sky opened and out of it fell rain, lightning, and thunder. While rain gushed down, lightning struck hard and caused thunder to react with a roar that scared the lizards and mamba snakes into hiding. Branches bobbed in the ferocious wind, leaves detached and scattered.

"Over there!" Ezomo yelled, pointing to a wooded area

speckled with fuchsia plants. "That's where I saw it."

Muja followed Ezomo's finger. "Hold this," Muja said, giving Ezomo the net. "When I throw the spear, you fling the net. That way, we'll trap him no matter what."

Ezomo studied the net. It was missing a few knots and tangled in some places. He frowned. "I . . . I . . . don't—"

"All you got to do is throw it. Nothing to it," Muja said, inching closer to the purple fuchsias. He raised the spear above his head and bent his right knee. Ezomo continued examining the net and wondered if it was big enough to cover a leopard. He lifted his head in time to see Muja charge forward and hurl the spear into a crown of young trees.

Ezomo froze and listened for the howling of a leopard. All he heard was rain beating the leaves and the scattering of small animals in the undergrowth.

Muja turned and looked at Ezomo. His eyes rested on the net still draped over Ezomo's arms. "What? You didn't throw it!"

Ezomo bowed his head. "I really am useless."

Muja gripped Ezomo's shoulders. "No. Just make sure you throw it next time!"

Ezomo nodded.

Chimama looked at Ezomo and Muja. "You think we—"

"*Shhh* . . ." said Muja. Parting wet branches and knotted climbers, he crept deeper into the grove, followed by Ezomo and Chimama. He stopped suddenly and frowned.

Peering over Muja's shoulders, Ezomo saw the spear lying on a mound of feathery grass.

"*Umph!* It got away," Muja said, slumping.

Chimama folded her arms. "We better go back. Too much rain."

Ezomo knelt and rubbed the soil with his hands. "Look!"

Muja hovered over Ezomo. "What?"

"Tracks," Ezomo said.

Muja squatted and brushed his thumb against the red earth. "Sure are! And there are more too." He pointed to deep indentations in the soil that led under a tunnel of palm leaves. "Good find," Muja said, patting Ezomo's back.

Ezomo inhaled deeply and clutched the net with both hands.

The friends followed the tracks. Thunder boomed above their heads. Rain washed their faces. They climbed a small slope and descended through weeds that scraped their shins. It was a matted mess of foliage to sift through, but soon their feet met a narrow dirt path that twisted and curved and led them to an area of the forest where dead marula trees lay scattered on the ground.

"Where the light go?" Chimama asked, gazing at the canopy of rotting branches tilting over the path. "Where are we?"

"They're gone," Muja said. "No more prints."

"The rain probably washed them away," said Ezomo.

"We better go home," Chimama said, scouting the area with wide eyes. "I don't know where we are."

Ezomo pointed. "Maybe it's hiding beyond there." He stepped over a trunk, edging in the direction he had pointed.

"Nothing looks familiar here." Muja scratched his head. "Why are all the plants dead?"

Chimama opened her fist, and the stone fell from her hand. "There's no leopard here!"

"Look!" Ezomo shouted. He dropped the net.

"What is it?" Muja asked, creeping through shadows.

"The . . . the . . . the village door," Ezomo whispered.

9

The Door

Ezomo moved carefully toward the door, like a predator sneaking up on its prey. Chimama and Muja followed to see for themselves the thing they had been warned about all their lives.

With lightning flashing around them, they stood gaping at the wooden structure nestled in a hedge of thorny bushes. The door was no taller than six feet. Its brownish-green front was made of eight planks. Fungi had chewed away the edges of the two middle planks, providing an opening for sedge weeds to squeeze through from the other side. A vine with velvety leaves drooped over the top and rested on a slab of decomposing wood affixed to the center of the door—the knob.

Chimama pressed her palm against her chest. "Don't open it!"

Muja's lips quivered. "If you see the door, run away. If you see the door, run away." He dropped the spear in the dirt.

Ezomo held his breath as he stared at the door.

Time waited patiently.

"We mustn't be here," Chimama said. "Oma warned—"

"It's real . . . ," Muja said, his voice shaking.

Behind them, something rustled in the bushes.

Ezomo spun around. "What was that?" He heard a whimper and saw dark spots darting between trees. "Over there!"

Muja shook his head, as if someone had splashed cold water on his face, and turned away from the door. He scooped up the spear, raised his arm, and bent his knees. Ezomo clenched the net with trembling hands and fixed his attention on the trees. Sharp green eyes glared back at Ezomo through drooping leaves. Lightning struck and illuminated the forest, followed by the crackling sound of a tree falling. Ezomo heard thunder roaring and felt the ground shake as the spear flew toward its target. It was in that moment, in a quiet space tucked between the raindrops, when everything went dark.

10

Something Is Wrong

Ezomo woke up in a puddle with his fist clamped around the net. The rain had stopped, and all around was silence— as if the forest had swallowed all the insects and all that remained were their muffled cries from inside its belly. He eased up to a seated position and rubbed the back of his head to soothe a sharp pain there. Then he scooched out of the muck and looked around, flinching when he saw the others. Chimama was curled up like a millipede, snoring. Beside her was Muja, lying flat on his back with deep lines occupying his forehead and a streak of spit oozing from the corner of his mouth.

Ezomo crawled over to Muja. "Wake up," he said, yanking Muja's arm.

The lines on Muja's forehead scrunched and straightened. His lips pursed.

"Wake up!"

Muja blinked his eyes open and sat up. "Was I asleep?"

"Your eyes were closed."

"Where's the leopard?" Muja asked.

Ezomo stared at the underbrush where he'd last seen the leopard. "Don't know. We should find it."

"Get up!" Muja said, tapping Chimama's arm. "We got to find the leopard."

Chimama opened her eyes and smiled lazily. Then her eyelids dropped to a close.

"Hey!" Muja yelled. "Wake up!"

Chimama was slow to sit. "What is it eh?" she said. Then she gasped.

"What's the matter with you?" Muja asked, puzzled.

"Look!" she said, pointing. "The village door—it's open."

Ezomo and Muja followed Chimama's finger to an awning of tree branches beyond which stood the village door, cracked open.

Chimama turned to Muja. "Did you open the door?"

Muja sprung up. "Of course not!"

"Then who did?"

Muja's eyes darted around and settled on the puddle. "Ezomo! You didn't throw the net again!" He dashed to the muddy water and scooped up the net to examine it. "You let the leopard get away!" He flung the net down.

"I . . . I . . . we . . ." Ezomo covered his mouth with his palm and then uncovered it quickly to speak. "The leopard must have escaped through the door when everything went dark . . . when we fell asleep."

"How come we fell asleep?" asked Chimama.

Ezomo rubbed his forehead. "Don't know."

Muja glowered at Ezomo. "If you'd just thrown the—"

"Thomething is wrong," Chimama said and stood up. "We betta leave."

"What about the leopard?" Ezomo asked.

Chimama placed both hands on her hips. "What about it?"

"Aren't we going to capture it?"

Chimama's eyes widened. "No! We're already in big trouble!"

Ezomo bowed his head, then quickly lifted it again to ask Chimama another question. "What about the door?"

"What about it?"

"Shouldn't we close it?"

Chimama stroked her chin. "You do it!"

"Me? Why me?"

"Eh? Is it not for you that Muja and I came here?"

Ezomo stared at the door. The muscles in his neck tightened. He bowed his head and fidgeted with his wrapper.

"Coward!" Chimama said.

"I'll do it," said Muja.

"Good," Chimama said. "Go then."

Muja crept toward the door. "We can't tell anybody about this," he said, looking back at Chimama and Ezomo.

"No—we can't," Chimama said.

"Swear it!"

Chimama shot Ezomo a scornful look. "Don't tell anybody." She turned to Muja. "We swear."

Muja inched closer to the door. He pinched his nose. "Eeww, it stinks!"

"Do it!" Chimama yelled.

Muja extended his right hand, and with his fingertips grabbed the decomposing knob and pulled. The door creaked to a close.

"He did it," Chimama whispered and smiled.

Muja beamed as he strutted past Ezomo. "Useless boy . . ." he mumbled.

II

Three Days to Live

Ezomo, Muja, and Chimama trudged out of the forest, saying nothing to each other. By the time they reached the village, the late afternoon had settled in for its shift and kept a gloomy gaze over Sesa.

"Where have all the birds gone?" Chimama asked as they passed the Palaver Hut and noticed that there were no kingfishers perched on the towering fever trees.

"Bisa!" Muja yelled.

There was no response.

When they got near the main compound, Ezomo, Chimama, and Muja saw people standing in a ring listening to Sao the orator speak. Some villagers stood on buckets and pots to see above the heads of others.

"They having meeting eh?" said Chimama, craning her neck.

As they got closer, they saw four women spreading their lappas on the ground, and two men wrestling to bind a goat.

"They're preparing a death ritual," Muja said.

Chimama winced. "For who?"

Above the bleating of the goat, Ezomo thought he heard someone say ". . . happened to Yatta," but he couldn't be sure.

"What they say happened to your mother?" Muja asked.

Ezomo looked around at the crowd. He saw tears and sad expressions, mouths whispering and mumbling, the women consoling each other. Ezomo bolted out of the main compound and toward his hut.

When Ezomo got there, men, women, and children were gathered in front. Some stood around murmuring. Others crowded the entryway and peered inside. A few sat on the damp ground looking somber.

"What's going on?" Ezomo asked no particular person. No one responded.

He thrust himself into the group of people standing by

the doorway and attempted to inch his way inside, but the crowd was thick and impossible to pierce. He crouched down and crawled under the tail of a lappa but could go no farther because people's feet were stubborn and refused to shuffle. He jumped to see above heads, but many of the villagers were taller than his jump, so he saw nothing.

Ezomo squeezed back out of the crowd and dashed around the hut. On one side was a small hole he had neglected to patch. Peeking inside, he saw that his hut was filled with the women who lived in his compound and two Elders. His eye darted around and settled on someone lying on the ground. It was his mother. She was curled up in a ball, and several of the women were rubbing her body with a white paste. Her face was pale too, and her lips were parted as if she was waiting on someone to pour water into her mouth. One woman held Yatta's head and fumbled with a black head wrap.

Ezomo clutched his chest. He placed his mouth against the hole. "Mamie!" He pressed his eye against the hole again and saw that Yatta was still on the ground, the women applying paste to her body.

Chimama tapped Ezomo's shoulder. "Is Yatta okay?"

"Mamie!" Ezomo yelled again before placing his ear against the hole. What he heard was not his mother's voice, but the voice of someone whispering: ". . . will die in a few days . . . when the moon reaches full."

Ezomo glanced up. Hidden between the branches of the tall palm trees was a clear sky holding a pale moon that was hard to see in the afternoon light. He stretched his eyes and saw that the moon was close to full. It would continue growing, becoming bigger, eating more light from the sun until its face was finally stuffed. "Three days," he murmured.

"Three days for what?" Chimama asked.

"Before the full moon."

"Is Yatta all right?" Muja asked, running up to them.

Ezomo didn't respond. He pressed his lips against the hole. "Mamie!" The women in the hut paid him no mind, and neither did Yatta. He slumped to the ground, buried his head in his lap, and wept.

Chimama sat beside Ezomo and placed her arm over his shoulders. He raised his head and rested it on his knees. His mother was going to die, just like his father. He sniffed the air and was certain he smelled death lingering—it smelled stale and sour.

He thought about how heartless some of the villagers were after the leopard had killed his father. They had mourned with him and Yatta a few days. They had wept and torn their hair. But thereafter, their visits had been to inquire about his father's debts. When Yatta could no longer pay, they took the one goat his family owned and threatened to take his father's wheelbarrow. Ezomo wondered what they would take from him when his mother was gone.

"*Umph*. Poor Yatta," said Muja, removing his eye from the hole. He sat down beside Ezomo and pressed his back against the wall of the hut.

Sitting between his only friends, Ezomo dried his eyes with his fingertips. He rested his head on Chimama's shoulder.

Chimama stroked Ezomo's head. "Is Yatta ill?"

Ezomo swallowed hard. "She's dying."

Chimama and Muja exchanged somber glances.

"Why?" Chimama asked, looking worried.

"Because of me," Ezomo said. "Because I make her cry. Now she's going to die."

"So—you will have no mother or father?" Muja asked.

Ezomo didn't answer.

"Maybe it isn't your fault. Maybe she caught rain fever," Muja said.

Ezomo shook his head. "No. I'm certain it's my fault."

"Can't be your fault," Chimama said firmly. She stood and peered through the hole in the side of the hut. "Thomething odd is happening."

"What do you mean?" Muja said.

Chimama looked at Muja. "Why the day Ezomo finds the leopard that killed his father, Yatta gets ill? Why didn't Yatta get ill yesterday eh? Or any other day except for the day Ezomo finds the leopard?" she asked.

"*Umph!* That's strange-o," said Muja, standing up.

"And who opened the village door eh?" Chimama whispered. "And why we fell asleep in the middle of hunting the leopard?"

"The sleeping thing was weird," Muja said.

Chimama knelt beside Ezomo and gripped his shoulders. "When did your father die?"

"Three years, two months, and . . ." Ezomo gasped.

Chimama shook Ezomo's shoulders. "What?"

". . . today!"

"Aha!" Chimama exclaimed. "The leopard came back

for your mother on the anniversary of your father's death!"

Ezomo pressed his palms against his cheeks. "But why?"

Chimama paced back and forth. "Witchcraft!"

Muja wagged his finger at Ezomo. "Should have trapped that leopard with the net. Then he wouldn't have come after your mother."

"That leopard put a spell on Yatta," Chimama said, still pacing.

"You think he put a spell on my father too?" Muja asked Chimama.

"For sure! He took your father's voice."

"What would the leopard want with my father's voice?"

"Remember the tale about the lizard?"

"What lizard?" Ezomo asked.

Chimama reminded Ezomo and Muja about a story Old Man Flomo had once told about a jealous lizard. Lizard was jealous of all the birds in the forest. He thought it was unfair that the birds could fly wherever they wanted while he was confined to the forest floor. Why did he have to slither on dirt while the birds soared in the sky? One morning, while all the animals slept, Lizard climbed a tree and stole the wings of a young bird sleeping in her nest. When the bird woke up and saw that her wings were gone, she cried so much that Sun felt sorry for her and decided to intervene. After searching the forest for days, Sun found Lizard hiding under a banana leaf holding the wings. Sun snatched the wings and gave them back to the bird so that she could be happy. Then Sun scolded Lizard and burned his head and tail. Now the jealous Lizard slithers around the forest with an orange head and tail.

"The leopard is jealous like the lizard," Chimama said.

"What is the leopard jealous about?" Ezomo asked.

Chimama shrugged. "I don't know but he's taking his jealousy out on us."

"So the leopard is the reason I live in Noroad?" Muja asked.

"Yeth!" Chimama said assuredly.

Muja clenched his fists. He frowned then asked, "You think the leopard has something to do with your mother's bad cooking?"

Chimama scrunched her face in thought.

"When did Chima stop cooking?" Muja asked.

"I don't remember. But bet the leopard has thomething to do with it," said Chimama with growing certainty.

Ezomo stood and faced Chimama. "So you think the leopard is the reason my mother is dying? Not me?"

"Yes!" Muja answered for Chimama. "And the reason my father can't speak, and Chimama's mother can't cook. That leopard is after our parents."

"But why *our* parents?" Ezomo asked.

"You know what we need to do?" Muja said.

Ezomo raised his eyebrows. "What?"

Muja leaned in. "We need to find out more about the leopard."

"But how? He went behind the . . ." Chimama looked around and lowered her voice. "Village door."

"Follow me," Muja said, dashing toward the front of the hut.

"Where we going?" Ezomo called after Muja.

"I know what to do!" Muja yelled.

Ezomo and Chimama looked at each other, and then they hurried after Muja to find out what exactly he knew.

12

A Plan to Help Us

"**Where** we going eh?" Chimama asked finally. They had been walking awhile on the dirt path along the river, and they were all beginning to feel tired and hungry. A cool evening breeze blew the wild ryegrass growing by the riverbank. Ezomo listened to the soft whistle of the wind and drew swirling patterns in his mind.

"I told you already. I got a plan," Muja said without slowing down. He had plucked a piece of ryegrass and was chewing on the stem.

"What kind of plan?" Chimama asked.

"A plan to help us."

Ezomo and Chimama exchanged glances.

"Is the plan nearby?" asked Chimama.

"No," said Muja.

"Where is it then?" asked Ezomo.

Muja halted and sighed loudly. He looked around to make sure no one was listening. A few fishing boats lingered across the river, but there were no fishermen in sight, and the women with babies tied to their backs who sold eels on the bank were elsewhere.

Muja wrung his hands. "We're going to the Valley to see Ada."

Chimama gasped. "The Valley!"

Muja slapped his palm on Chimama's mouth. "*Shhh . . .*"

Chimama peeled Muja's hand away. "Have you gone mad!"

"Listen to me," Muja said, leaning close to Ezomo and Chimama. First he talked about his father's inability to speak and how shameful it was that Toba was no longer allowed to hunt. He pantomimed his father sitting mum under a palm tree. How he longed for his father to take him hunting once again! If his father could speak, his family would be allowed to live in Passtru, and he could reclaim respect from the other boys in the village. If his father could speak, he would be allowed to sit in the middle row under the mango tree. He smiled at the thought.

Next, Muja reminded Chimama about her mother's inability to cook and how shameful it was for Chima to be the only woman in Sesa who wasn't allowed to add food to a single pot under the Palaver Hut. He carried on about the many dishes Chima attempted to prepare, and all the mushy substances that tasted so bitter or salty that Chimama had to rely on neighbors to eat a decent meal. Chimama avoided Muja's eyes as he spoke and fidgeted with a loose thread on her lappa. If Chima could cook, Muja said, the other girls would stop taunting her—they would stop saying that no boy would marry her. If Chima could cook, Chimama would be allowed to sit in the middle row under the mango tree.

"And you," Muja said, pointing to Ezomo. "If Yatta dies, what will the Elders do to you?"

Ezomo bowed his head.

"What that got to do with the Valley and Ada eh?" Chimama said, scratching the top of her head.

"Don't you understand? That leopard is after *our* parents, and we don't know why. That leopard is the reason my father can't speak, and your mother can't cook. It killed

Ezomo's father, and now it's after his mother. Unless we capture that leopard, it will continue to haunt us." Muja grabbed Chimama's hand. "Maybe Ada knows something about the leopard. Maybe the leopard was the evil thing that happened to Sesa when Ada opened the village door."

Chimama bit her bottom lip. "No! We can't go to the Valley." She yanked her hand from Muja's grip. "Oma will find out."

"Who will tell Oma?"

The three friends looked at each other.

"What about the big bats?" Chimama said with arms stretched wide. "Remember what Oma told us?"

Muja chuckled incredulously. "You're scared of bats?"

Chimama crossed her arms. "Ada probably knows nothing about the leopard."

"Do you want to keep living in Noroad and see shame in your mother's eyes all your life?" Muja said, wagging his finger.

"No. But I don't want to go the Valley either." Chimama turned away and began walking back the way they had come.

Muja lowered his head and followed her.

Ezomo watched them go, his heart pounding. Quickly, he knelt and filled his trembling palm with mud. Then he stood and raised his arm. "Wait!" he shouted as the ball of mud left his palm.

"Have you gone mad too!" Chimama said when the muck smacked the back of her head, and she saw that it was Ezomo who had flung it.

Ezomo wiped his eyes and stared at Chimama. "Her knuckles bleed."

Chimama tilted her head. "Wetin you talking about?" She walked back to Ezomo.

Ezomo showed Chimama his knuckles. "My mother . . . her knuckles bleed. And at night, she doesn't sleep—just stays up crying. Hasn't she suffered enough? Please don't let her die." A tear waddled down his cheek. "Ada might know something about the leopard that can save her."

Chimama sighed heavily. "All right! We'll go. But we can't linger."

"We won't," Muja said. "We'll ask a few questions and leave."

"No! Only one question. Nothing more!" Chimama stamped her foot.

"Okay. Only one question," agreed Muja.

"Promithe?"

"I promise."

When the three of them had agreed to the plan, Muja pointed to the bald hills in the distance. Ezomo's eyes followed Muja's finger along the river and down the dirt path that twisted and narrowed into a forsaken stretch of road hardly anyone traveled because it led to the Valley, a place reserved for villagers who had committed the most heinous crimes.

"Let's race. Last one to reach the hills is a monkey butt!" Muja said and took off without waiting for his friends to agree.

"Eeww!" Chimama exclaimed, running after Muja.

Ezomo glanced up at the pale moon. His mother still had three days to live. Then he raced after Chimama and Muja, who were already sprinting toward the hills.

13

Who Is Ada?

Muja was the first to reach the hills, followed by Chimama. Last was Ezomo, and when he arrived, he collapsed on the ground panting.

"Monkey butt!" Muja said to Ezomo.

Chimama giggled. "Monkey butt!" She huffed and puffed.

Ezomo sat up and looked around. The river and palm trees had given way to a steep terrain with rocky red soil and wilted bulbine plants. Adjacent to the hills was a road that stretched to more barren hills in the distance. A low whistle blew from the mouth of the wind and filled the silent spaces.

"This place is creepy," Chimama said, scanning the area.

Muja pointed to the road. "The Valley is over—"

Trrrrr . . .

Muja flinched. "Did you hear that?"

"Look!" Chimama shouted.

Ezomo and Muja followed her finger to see an object in the sky hurtling toward them.

"What's that?" Muja said. He grabbed a stone from the ground.

"A bat!" Chimama turned and ran back toward the river. Ezomo and Muja followed her, but soon the thing was directly above their heads.

"It's just a bird!" Muja yelled, slowing himself to a stop. He dropped the stone.

"I'm not *just* a bird," the bird said, landing near Muja's feet. "My name is Humongous. Humongous from the Forsaken Valley." The bird spoke in a deep and distinguished voice, like a wise grandfather.

Ezomo and Chimama stopped running. Chimama walked back toward Muja and the bird. Ezomo followed her.

"Humongous from the Forsaken Valley?" Muja asked.

"Yes, that's me," the bird said and stretched his neck with pride.

Muja circled the bird. It was a petite kingfisher, no bigger than Muja's palm, with black-and-white feathers and a large red bill. "Why you call yourself Humongous when you so small?"

The bird frowned. "Because I have big job."

"What big job?" asked Muja.

"I alert the forsaken people when the Elders are coming," said the bird.

"Why?"

"Because that's what I do." Humongous puffed out his chest feathers.

"What they do when the Elders are coming?"

"Nothing."

"Not a big job at all," Muja muttered.

Humongous tapped his foot, waiting for another question from Muja, but this time the question came from Ezomo.

"Do you know Ada?"

"Who is that?" Humongous said while looking Ezomo up and down.

The children glanced at one another.

"The girl who opened the village—"

"Oooh, that girl." Humongous nodded. "We don't call her Ada no more."

"What you call her?" Chimama asked.

"Old Woman."

Chimama raised her eyebrows. "Old Woman?"

"Yes, she's very old."

"So you know her?" Ezomo asked.

"Of course I know her."

"She's real?"

"Of course she's real."

Ezomo let out a big breath. "Can you take us to her?"

Humongous covered his face with his wing and shook his head. "No! She's not available."

Muja's eyes bulged. "Why not? We have to see her!"

Humongous uncovered his face and said, "If you want see forsaken people, there are many others in the Valley who will do. How about the man who tried to steal the sun? Or the woman who tried to burn down the Palaver Hut? You want see them?"

Chimama grabbed Muja's arm. "Let's go home. Ada is not available."

Muja yanked his arm from Chimama's grip. "We don't

want to see those people," he snapped at the bird. "We want to see Ada!"

"How about me?" asked the bird. "I'm forsaken and right here for you to see."

"What did *you* do?" Chimama asked.

The bird gazed at the distant hills. "Too sinful for your childish ears to hear."

Muja rolled his eyes. "Where did Ada go?"

"Nowhere! She just don't see visitors no more."

"Others have come to see her?" Ezomo asked.

"No. You're the first."

"Then how you know she don't see visitors?" Muja asked.

"I just do!" Humongous flapped his wings, preparing to fly away.

"Wait!" Ezomo croaked. "But . . . but . . . my mother will die if we don't see Ada."

Humongous stared at Ezomo. "What you say?"

"My mother will die," repeated Ezomo. "They say she will die when the moon turns full."

The bird hopped in front of Ezomo and looked him up and down. "And how will seeing Old Woman help your mother?"

"We want to find out what Ada knows about the leopard," Ezomo explained.

"That leopard is the reason my father can't speak, and Chimama's mother can't cook. It killed Ezomo's father, and now it's trying to kill his mother," Muja said.

"Oooooh . . . I see," Humongous said, walking a circle around the three friends. "How old are you children?"

"Ten. I'll be eleven soon," Ezomo said.

"Yes, soon he'll be a man like me!" Muja poked Ezomo and laughed. "I'm eleven. Chimama is nine."

"You mean all three of you are . . . Well!" Humongous said with a smile. "Wait here. I'll go tell Old Woman you want to see her."

Ezomo, Chimama, and Muja watched Humongous take off and disappear into the lilac sky.

"That was some odd bird," said Muja.

"Very odd," agreed Chimama.

They sat by a hill to wait.

"Let's play a game," Muja said, tossing a pebble in the air. He grabbed three stones from the ground before catching the pebble.

"Only three? I can grab more," Chimama challenged.

"You'll grab zero," Muja said, handing Chimama the pebble.

Chimama tossed the pebble and grabbed five stones before catching the pebble again. "Told you I could get more!"

"You got lucky."

"You try," Chimama said, giving the pebble to Ezomo. "Bet you'll grab more than Muja."

Ezomo tossed the pebble in the air, but just as he reached to grab stones, he heard rattling in the sky.

Trrrrr . . .

"Here he comes!" Chimama shouted.

Ezomo stood up and watched the little bird flying toward them. He fixed his gaze on the stone-covered path that led to the Valley, and as far as he could see, no Old Woman was trailing the bird by foot.

"Where is Ada?" Ezomo asked when Humongous landed near his feet.

"She say come back at night. When moon is shining bright, she will see you."

"So she can help us?" Muja asked.

"Yes. She can help you," Humongous said.

Ezomo let out a sigh of relief.

"But—children are not allowed to leave their hut at night without their mother or father," Chimama said.

Humongous flapped his wings. "Children also aren't allowed this close to the Valley. Come back at night or don't come back at all," he said and flew away.

"We can't go out at night!" yelled Chimama. "No way!"

Muja rubbed the back of his neck. "We've already broken two rules. What's one more? No one will ever find out."

"Oma might find out!" Chimama argued.

"Who will tell her?" asked Muja.

Chimama stamped her foot. "Bitha will."

"Oh, yes, Bisa," Muja said. "Cantankerous bird!"

Ezomo cleared his throat and spoke softly. "Ada must know something about the leopard. I will come back at night if it means saving my mother. If you want to help your parents, you should come too." Then Ezomo turned away from his two friends and headed for home.

14
Tonight

Ezomo sat in the corner of his hut, hugging his leg and watching his mother gasp for air like a fish forgotten on the riverbank. He mirrored her breathing—when she breathed in, so did he. When she breathed out, he did too. Two women from his compound, one named Benu and the other named Mina, sat beside Yatta and took turns dabbing her forehead with a wet rag while lamenting the declining crops and grumbling about the sun's refusal to shine and all the problems it caused the villagers. The oil lamp sat in the middle of the room, and out of it beamed a yellow light whose glow flickered on their faces as they talked. Benu and Mina attended to Yatta without speaking to Ezomo. Even when they ate rice and fish which a small boy named Obu delivered, they offered Ezomo nothing but sorrowful looks.

"Good thing the father not here to see this," Mina said.

"Fool! If the father was alive, this wouldn't happen," Benu argued while stuffing her mouth with rice.

Mina rose to her feet and looked slowly around the hut. With her arms extended, she walked in a circle around Yatta, feeling for something Ezomo couldn't see. Then she stopped with her back facing Ezomo and whispered, "The body is dying, but the spirit is alive and here with us. We must remain hopeful." She made another circle around Yatta before sitting down. Benu nodded. Then the two women sat staring at the bobbing light until all the oil in the lamp dissipated, and darkness permeated the hut and compelled them to sleep. Moving quietly, Ezomo kissed Yatta's wet forehead and left.

Outside, Ezomo saw cheerful flames flickering from inside several huts, casting a dim light on the otherwise dark compound. A thin streak of smoke rose from a doused firepit, and Ezomo heard the cry of a restless baby in the distance. Standing just outside his doorway, he marveled at the dark night sky. The last time he remembered being out at night was when his father was alive. It had been during harvest season when the crops had to be transported from farm to market, and his father had taken him along to help tote the load.

His parents had warned him many times not to visit the night alone. The Elders and Oma had too. Even the child with the most promise was senseless at night and required the oversight of a mature person. In the beginning, this rule was only mildly enforced. When a child broke it, there were meager consequences, if any at all. That was before a boy named Ofasa went out alone one night and did a terrible thing. Thereafter, the Elders proclaimed that any child who left their hut at night without a parent would be sent to the Valley.

A breeze rushed by and brushed Ezomo's face. He inhaled the air and released it through his nose. Then he tiptoed around to the back of his hut and stood in the wild grass with eyes stretched wide to see beyond the blackness that accosted him.

He stood with his back pressed against the mud wall until he'd mustered enough courage to step forward into the darkness. The sounds of crickets chirping in the grass sassed in his ears as he crept through the wooded outskirts of his compound. Trampling wild ferns and poison ivy, he moved carefully, his arms extended to feel his way through the thick vegetation.

The groans of bullfrogs joined the chirping of crickets as Ezomo scrambled down a steep slope where the rain had eaten away the land and left a deep indentation in the soil. He eased forward until a hare foraging for food brushed against his leg. Ezomo jumped and yelped, then quickly covered his mouth. He knew for certain that if anyone found him, he would be sent to the Valley, and his mother would die.

After catching his breath, Ezomo kept on, heart pounding and legs trembling. He scrambled up a small hill and turned right onto the narrow road. Soon the thick bushes on either side of the road were joined by small trees, and Ezomo zigzagged between them, forging ahead.

He had just regained small courage when something scaly slithered over his foot, and he froze to let the thing cross. Tears welled up in his eyes, and he rubbed them away with the back of his hand. Sensing that he was near the Noroad compound because of the distance he had walked and the appearance of palm trees, he took a deep breath and ran full speed through the foliage. He only let the air escape his mouth when he heard sobbing.

Ezomo rested his hands on his knees and gasped. He recognized the cry. It was the kind of cry that blossomed in the heart, endured suppression in the throat, and forced its way out of the mouth in weak vibrations. It was the same way Yatta cried at night when she thought he was asleep. Suddenly, he heard quick steps approaching from the left. He ducked.

"It's me," hissed a voice.

Ezomo spotted Muja waving at him from behind a palm tree, the hunting bag around his waist. He rushed to hug him.

"Get off me—" Muja pushed Ezomo away. He thumped Ezomo's shoulder with his fist and smiled.

"Where is Chimama?" Ezomo whispered.

Muja looked around. "She was supposed to meet us here." Panic rested on his face. "She probably fell asleep. We have to go get her."

Ezomo pointed to a small fire burning in the compound. "We can't. Someone's awake."

The Noroad compound where Chimama and Muja

lived consisted of flimsy shacks made from twigs and palm branches. Next to the cluster of shacks was a small gazebo where the residents kept community cooking pots and pans. Across from the gazebo was the wooded area where Ezomo and Muja, hidden, stood gazing at the fire.

Ezomo spotted Chimama's mother, Chima, hovering over the blaze. She was using a long wooden stick to stir something in a pot. The cry he had heard was coming from her. Ezomo stared with an open mouth, surprised to see the woman who so often bullied others crying like a small child. "What she doing?" he whispered.

"Cooking," Muja said.

"At night?"

"She waits until the others are asleep. Then she comes out and tries to cook."

"Poor Chima," Ezomo whispered.

Muja grabbed Ezomo's arm. "Come on . . . we need to get Chimama."

"How?" Ezomo asked, pointing to the gazebo. "Chima will see us."

"If we're quiet, she won't," whispered Muja.

"She *will*."

Muja frowned. "Thought you were ready to be brave."

Ezomo didn't say another word, and instead crept into the yard. Muja followed closely behind.

They crawled like lizards behind some palm trees, over dead fronds scattered across the muddy ground. As they approached the gazebo, they slowed their pace. Ezomo's heart pounded. Sweat dripped down the sides of his face. Muja's lips trembled. His eyes bulged.

Chima had her back to them, and Ezomo and Muja hoped she wouldn't turn around, for there was nothing for them to hide behind. On their bellies they slithered, their shadows moving cautiously with them. Ezomo did not see the old drum lying in the dirt, and when his elbow brushed against the instrument, it boomed.

"Who's there?" Chima asked the night.

Ezomo froze. On the ground beside him, Muja held his breath.

Chima turned to her left. She turned to her right. She spun around and stared at the place where Ezomo and Muja lay in the dark. "Who goes there?"

Behind Chima, something shuffled into the light, revealing itself to be a man. "What are you doing, Chima?" the man said. Chima turned her back to the boys and hurried to douse the fire.

"It's Chimama's father," Muja whispered to Ezomo. "Why is he awake?"

Ezomo and Muja scampered to the safety of a hibiscus bush and watched Chimama's parents put out the fire and, murmuring, leave the gazebo.

"They're probably going home," Ezomo whispered.

"We must reach Chimama before they do," Muja said.

Ezomo and Muja scurried under a clothesline bearing damp lappas, slipped past a well, and sprinted toward Chimama's shack. Above their heads, the moon watched on.

The two boys peered between the twigs and palm branches that were their friend's home. They saw Chimama sleeping soundly inside. Muja tiptoed to the entryway and threw a pebble at her. It landed on Chimama's stomach and produced no reaction.

He threw another pebble. Chimama shifted onto her right side, made a pillow out of her arms, and resumed snoring.

"Chimama!" Muja whisper-shouted.

Ezomo filled his palm with red earth. Then he flung it. It

landed on Chimama's face. She sat up and shook her head.

Muja smiled and thumped Ezomo's shoulder. Ezomo's upper lip curled into an almost smile.

Rubbing her forehead, Chimama looked around sleepily and froze when she spotted Ezomo and Muja. She widened her eyes and smiled.

"Your parents are on their way here," Muja whispered.

"Quick, help me cover the bag of rice like we planned," Chimama said, pointing to a sack in the corner of her hut.

After Ezomo, Muja, and Chimama had quickly covered the bag of rice with a blanket, they tiptoed out of the hut and raced away from the compound. Ezomo smiled when they were in the clear. Chimama and Muja hugged each other. They had never been out alone at night, and they were excited and afraid. Indeed, there was plenty to fear. Sleepless villagers often roamed the paths at night. And above them were the watchful eyes of the kingfisher birds. Nevertheless, the friends had courage in their hearts, and hope too, so they scurried among the shadows and hurried forward into the dark night.

15

Take Us to the Valley

Ezomo, Muja, and Chimama decided to approach the Valley by way of the farm. They scurried on rarely used paths, ducking at the slightest noise.

"Too bad they don't let us out alone at night eh?" Chimama whispered, looking at the stars twinkling in the sky. "It's so beautiful. . . ."

"Ofasa ruined it for us all," said Muja, kicking the dirt.

Ofasa was a young boy who many years earlier had left his hut in the middle of the night to get a drink of water. Standing by the water drum, he'd filled a bowl and drunk until a firefly playing in the grass caught his attention. Ofasa watched the firefly dart around and decided he wanted a shining tail too. He returned to his hut and retrieved a rag.

Back outside, he twisted the rag until it resembled a thick piece of rope. Then he lit one end on fire and chased the firefly around the grass. Ofasa was having so much fun pretending to be a lightning bug that he didn't see the sparks fly from the rag and catch the grass on fire. By the time he noticed, the fire had spread across the grass and was growing fast. He stamped on the rag and ran to call his parents. It took his mother and father a while to wake up, and when they finally did, the fire was uncontainable. A herd of goats died, and fifteen huts had to be rebuilt. The Elders deliberated Ofasa's fate for several days and decided to send him to the Valley. The villagers pleaded for Ofasa, and his mother and father wept like babies. Ofasa's grandmother held the Elders' feet and cried like a child, but nothing changed their minds. They said that Ofasa could have destroyed Sesa and therefore had to be severely punished despite his age. Thereafter, the rule of no child going out alone at night was strictly enforced. Any child seen outside at night without a parent would be sent straight to the Valley.

When Ezomo, Muja, and Chimama reached the farm, they hid behind Oma's mango tree and surveyed the area. The farm was deserted. Only a forgotten fruit basket lingered. The shadows of branches bobbed. Leaves rustled when a breeze blew from across the river. Ezomo took a deep breath and filled his nostrils with the smell of ripe mangos.

"The field is empty," Muja announced. "We'll go across it to the river and then we'll walk to the Valley. We're half-way there."

"I'm tired. Got to rest a bit," Chimama whispered and plopped on the ground.

Muja picked up a twig and wagged it at Chimama, imitating Oma. "You can sit in the front row today," he said.

Chimama covered her mouth and giggled, then with her chin held high and arms swinging, she walked to the spot usually reserved for children with bloodlines to the Elders and sat down.

Muja wagged the stick at Ezomo. "And you fine boy," he said, "you can sit anywhere you want."

Ezomo crossed his arms and stared blankly at Muja.

Muja pushed Ezomo away from the trunk of the mango tree. "Go!"

Hesitantly, Ezomo sat beside Chimama.

Muja stood before his pupils. "Where is that Muja? He

needs to pay his school fees," he said, still pretending to be Oma.

Chimama raised her hand. "I'll pay for Muja," she said, giggling.

Ezomo glanced at the moon. It was pale yellow with shadowy splotches and a dim side where the light had not yet spread. He stood up. "We better get going. Still got far to go."

"You're right," Chimama said, standing up. "We have to return home before daybreak. Let's go!"

They ran across the fields toward the river.

Ezomo, Chimama, and Muja hurried along the dirt path next to the river, arms locked to keep warm, ears listening to waves bumping against the bank. They walked past the bald hills and continued down the rocky road leading to the Valley. Barren leadwood trees appeared here and there, but aside from that, there was nothing to see but more hills in the distance.

They walked until they reached the middle of the night— when the beginning of the night was too far behind to turn back, and the end of the night wasn't near enough to reach for.

"I hope Yatta won't die," Chimama said. She placed her arm over Ezomo's shoulders. "If Yatta die, you can live with me."

"*Umph!* Don't live with her-o," Muja said. "You will die from starvation."

"Fool! Do I look hungry to you?" Chimama said, gripping her stocky belly.

Muja laughed. "Your neighbors won't feed you forever Chimama. One day, you'll have to cook for your family."

Chimama shook her head. "Won't be happening."

"Why don't you cook, Chimama?" Ezomo asked.

"She's afraid to! She thinks her food will be worse than her mother's," Muja said.

Chimama glared at Muja. "Thtop it!"

"Listen!" Ezomo exclaimed. "I hear something."

Trrrrr . . . Trrrrr . . .

"It's Humongous!" Muja shouted, looking around.

They spotted the blur of a bird soaring toward them. It flew fast and straight, like an arrow destined to reach its target.

"You frisky little children!" Humongous said once he landed. "You really came!"

"Of course we came!" Muja boasted.

"Of course you did! When an impala is starving, it will visit a lion's den to find food," Humongous said, unfolding his wings. "What brave children you are."

"How we get to Ada?" Muja asked.

Humongous pointed to the dark shapes of hills in the distance. "That way! We'll cross a big field, and then there will be a cliff. Below the cliff is Old Woman's hill." He flapped his wings and ascended into the sky. "Follow me!"

They followed Humongous across the field, and then stopped, realizing that they could no longer see the bird.

"Where is he?" asked Ezomo.

"Right here!" Humongous had reappeared. "Keep up!"

They zigzagged between stones, stopping when they could no longer see Humongous and continuing when he circled back.

"What about the big bats?" Chimama whispered.

"Don't worry about bats," Muja said. "I won't let them harm you."

Ezomo was silent. He kept his gaze on the bird and his feet at a steady pace, doing his best to keep up. His eyes glinted. He felt terrified, but brave too, for though the night was dark and dangerous and filled with uncertainty, the night was also exciting and filled with promise, for he was with his two friends and they were after the leopard that killed his father, and it was possible, very much so, that he, useless and all, could save his dying mother.

16

Sliding Down

Humongous tapped his two-toed foot on an enormous kapok tree that tilted down from the rim of the cliff toward the Valley which stretched below them like the jaws of a hungry lion. The trunk of the tree was split open with all the pulp removed so that it resembled a giant slide.

"Get in," Humongous said, pointing to the tree.

The friends looked at one another, eyes wide, then back at the kapok tree.

Muja shook his head. "We'll speak to Ada from here."

Humongous huffed. "Not possible."

"Why not?"

"Bad leg. She can't climb up."

Chimama's eyes bulged with fear. "We can't go down there."

"But we've come too far to turn back," Muja said, pacing back and forth.

Chimama crossed her arms and glared at Muja. "We are *not* going down there!"

Muja turned to Ezomo. "What you think?"

It was difficult to see in the darkness, but Ezomo could tell that they were standing above some kind of gorge. He inched to the edge of the cliff. He spotted a flame burning below and saw small figures moving around. From where he stood, the people, trees, and fire pit down below looked miniature.

"At least there aren't any bats," he said to Chimama.

"Chimama . . ." Muja grabbed her hand. "Aren't you tired sitting in the back row under the mango tree? Aren't you tired of being teased by the other girls?"

Chimama nodded.

"Then we have to go down and find out what Ada knows about the leopard."

Chimama hung her head and nodded again.

Muja pointed to the giant slide. "How we use it?"

Humongous rolled his eyes. Then he hopped into the kapok tree, sat down, and pushed himself forward with his wings. Ezomo, Chimama, and Muja watched him glide down until he reached the bottom. They could barely see him it was so far down.

"Easy enough," Muja said. "I'll go first."

"But—what if we can't get back up?" Chimama asked. "We need to get home before the night is over."

"Then at least we'll have each other. And we'll know we tried to help our parents," Muja said. He hugged Chimama. Then he looked Ezomo in the eyes. "We'll know we tried to save Yatta." He thumped Ezomo's shoulders. "You're braver than I thought."

Ezomo looked at his feet and fiddled with his wrapper.

Muja stepped into the trunk. He sat, squeezed his knees together, and gripped the rim of the slide.

"Better you close your eyes," Ezomo said.

Muja squeezed his eyes shut and pushed himself down.

"Can't watch," Chimama said, covering her eyes with the tail of her lappa.

Ezomo watched his friend slide down the tree. It reminded him of a raindrop gliding down a leaf. "He landed!"

Chimama uncovered her eyes and saw a tiny hand waving from below. "He did it," she whispered. "I'll go next.

Not going to be up here alone." She untied the knot on her lappa and tightened it. Then she climbed into the trunk and placed her hands neatly on her lap. "Give me a good push Ezomo," she said, closing her eyes.

Using both hands, Ezomo pushed Chimama's back and watched her glide down the tree. Halfway down, if anyone were watching, they would have seen a smile appear on Chimama's face. When she reached the bottom, she waved to Ezomo.

Ezomo looked at the slide. Then he looked up at the moon meshed between the clouds. He wondered if Benu and Mina were still with Yatta or if she was all alone. He looked behind him, in the direction from which they had come. The way home was far. Ezomo stepped in the kapok tree, sat down, and closed his eyes. He kept his eyes shut until his feet touched the ground again.

17

The Center Point

The Valley was cold and dim. Houses resembling giant ant-hills clustered in one area. Scrawny coconut trees clustered in another. Cutting through the gorge was a dry stream-bed filled with wild grass and witchweed. A committee of vultures pecked at something lying in the dirt. Moonlight brightened the shadows.

Even though it was the middle of the night, people came out of their anthills and gathered around Ezomo, Chimama, and Muja, examining them with ravenous eyes as if they were chunks of meat. The three friends stood close together facing the crowd. Ezomo's heart thumped fast, like drums during a ritual. He wondered if they were going to be eaten.

Chimama elbowed Muja. "Where'd the bird go?"

"Where is Humongous?" Muja asked. His question was answered with murmurs and confusion. A bony man extended his forefinger and touched Muja's face.

"Stop it!" Muja said with a trembling voice.

"Are they here? Where are they?"

The crowd parted, revealing a thin girl with matted hair and bright eyes standing in the entryway of an anthill. She wore a raggedy lappa, and around her neck was a string with a kola nut in the middle of it. As she came into the moonlight, they saw that her left leg was wrapped in a rag and in her left hand, she held a rattan stick. When her right leg stepped, the stick wobbled and stepped too. Humongous fluttered beside her.

"Who's that?" Ezomo whispered.

"Ada of course," Humongous said.

Ezomo's mouth fell open. "You said Ada was an old woman."

"Yes, in spirit, not body. People don't age in the Valley. Didn't Oma tell you? Ada's like a ripe banana still green."

Ada's eyes flickered from Ezomo to Chimama, then to Muja, back to Ezomo before returning to Chimama where they rested a short while and grew wide. She grinned, revealing a mouth full of brown teeth. "You're really here," she exclaimed. "How long was the walk? Did you see anyone? Did anyone see you? Sliding down the kapok tree was fun right? Don't you think so?" Her voice was in a hurry to reach somewhere, for it spoke quickly without rest and shoved words out of her mouth so that they bumped against each other as they fell from her lips.

"Did you stop to swim?" She went on. "Was the water warm? I love to swim. I can climb good too. Can you climb? What games do you like to play?" Her eyebrows lifted. "I know plenty games we can play."

Ezomo glanced at Muja and Chimama, and then said to Ada, "We came to—"

"You're Ezomo!" Ada interrupted, pointing at him.

"Yes."

"You're the one with the dying mother."

Ezomo nodded. His gaze strayed to the moon hanging in the sky. It was still the same size, but its pale color had thickened to a creamy yellow, like juice from a mango. He guided his eyes back to Ada.

"The Elders haven't sent any children to the Valley in a long time. How I've longed to see other children. Sit down,"

Ada said, pointing to a ring of rocks near her anthill.

Ezomo, Chimama, and Muja sat down.

"Ofasa . . . ," Ada called. "Bring my friends some water."

A small boy wearing a brown wrapper brought them murky water in a coconut shell.

"Ofasa is real?" Muja asked, staring at the boy scuttling toward them.

Ada giggled. "Of course he's real. Sit beside me, Ofasa." She spoke tenderly, like a mother speaking to a son.

Humongous hopped to the ring of rocks and perched on Ada's lap.

Ezomo, Chimama, and Muja passed around the coconut shell until they'd each had a sip of water. Ezomo noticed that some of the people had returned to their houses. Others sat on the ground and gawked at them.

"So! You've come to hear about the door?" asked Ada.

"Yes," said Muja. "We want to know if the leop—"

"I never intended to open the village door. It was an accident."

"What?" Chimama looked at Muja and Ezomo in disbelief.

"Back then, I was very curious. I wanted to know why

it rained, why the sky is blue, and why birds talk. But what I was most curious about . . ." Ada leaned toward them. "Was what lay behind our village door. It was the one question no one could answer. This made my bones ache terribly. . . ." Ada rubbed her hands over her chest and shoulders. "Sharp pains right here. Ever felt pain like that?" She carried on without waiting for an answer. "I tried to occupy my mind with things to distract me. I played the drums, went fishing with my father, helped my mother sell lappas in the market, and still, I couldn't stop thinking about the door. The ache in my bones was stubborn."

"What did you do?" Chimama asked.

"One night, while my father and mother slept, I left my hut."

Chimama's eyes stretched. "Where'd you go?"

"I walked to the forest. There I met Bisa."

Muja smacked his forehead. "Bisa is everywhere! Cantankerous bird! What he say?"

"He asked me what I was doing out at night without my parents."

"What you tell him?" Muja asked.

"The truth. My parents taught me not to lie." She paused and bowed her head solemnly. Then she looked up and said, "I told Bisa I was going to see what was behind the village door. He thought I was joking, so he laughed at me. But when he saw me walking into the forest, he pleaded with me not to go. He warned me that if I did, he would alert the Elders."

Ezomo frowned. "Why didn't you go home?"

"The ache in my bones was unbearable. I told him if I didn't open the door, the ache would kill me. I ran into the forest, the fastest I'd ever run. And I kept running until I was staring at the door."

"How did you know where the door was?" Ezomo asked.

Ada stroked Humongous. "My good friend told me."

"Told you I was sinful," Humongous said, flicking his tail up and down.

Muja rolled his eyes. "What happened next?"

"Bisa had followed me. He didn't believe I would do it. I considered what might happen to Sesa if I opened the door. I also wondered what the Elders would do to my mother and father. A different idea entered my mind."

"Ooooh . . . ?" Chimama bit her lip.

"I placed my ear against the door. I reasoned that by doing so, I would hear something and that would be enough to cure my ache, and I could return home and continue my life without bringing harm to the village. But as soon as I placed my ear against the door, it sprung open, just wide enough for me to see what was behind it."

Muja's eyes bulged. "What did you see?"

"Nothing at first, because I was chasing Bisa who was on his way to alert the Elders. But then I decided that since I was already in big trouble, I might as well see what was behind the door."

"You turned around and went back?" Chimama asked.

"I ran back. The door was cracked open just like I left it, so I slid my body through the little opening."

"Did you see the leopard?" Ezomo asked.

Ada scrunched her face. "What leopard?"

The children exchanged glances.

"The leopard Humongous said you knew all about," Muja said.

Ada tucked her lips into her mouth. Then untucked them quickly to say, "Oh yes. The leopard. I saw it."

Ezomo released the breath he was keeping.

"It's big," Ada said. "How did it get so big? It's scary too. Doesn't it look scary?"

Ezomo nodded. "Where did you see it?"

Ada took a sip of water, placed the shell on the ground, and folded her hands in her lap. "Behind the door. When I went. It's huge."

"Did you see its green eyes?" Muja asked.

Ada nodded. "Uh-huh."

"The leopard is witching our parents," Chimama said.

"It killed Ezomo's father, and now it's back to kill his mother," Muja added. "It even put a sleeping spell on us when we tried to capture it."

"And it's why my mother can't cook, and Muja's father can't talk."

Ada rubbed her chin. "What a bad, bad leopard."

"What else do you know about the leopard?" Ezomo said. "How does its magic work?"

The children waited as Ada took another sip of water. "It has powerful magic, that leopard. But don't worry. I know what to do." Her speech was slow now, as if she had lined up her words carefully in the back of her throat and was ushering them out of her mouth one by one. "I can make your mother cook," she said to Chimama. "Make your father speak," she said to Muja, "and cure your dying mother," she said to Ezomo.

"That's why we came!" Muja said, beaming. He leaned forward. "How exactly are you going to do that?"

"She can take you behind the village door to find the leopard," Humongous said.

Ada stroked the bird's head. "Yes, I can. I know where the leopard hides."

Chimama wagged her head. "No. We're not going behind the door. Never!"

"Isn't there some other way you can help us?" Ezomo pleaded. "We can't go behind the door."

"No other way." Ada clutched Ezomo's hand. "Do you want to lose your mother and father like I lost my mother and father?" She released her grip.

Ezomo's face softened. He recognized something in Ada's eyes that mirrored the feelings he'd carried for so long. Feelings that were powerful yet fragile—that filled him with shame and anxiety and compelled him to feel peace only in solitude.

"What happened to your mother and father?" Ezomo asked quietly.

Ada clenched her jaw. "When I returned to the village, the Elders were waiting for me. They said I had allowed evil into Sesa. They said all the baby goats and sheep died mysteriously the night I opened the door. They took me straight to the Valley—didn't even get a chance to say goodbye to my mother or father. I never saw them again. I miss them." She stood up. "We must hurry. The door is far."

Chimama stood and crossed her arms. "No. The Elders will find out we went behind the door."

"Who will tell them?" Ada asked.

Chimama frowned. "Bitha will! He will see us when we walk by."

"I know another way," Ada said.

"Told you she's wise," Humongous said.

Chimama wasn't convinced. "What if thomething evil happens when we open the door?"

Ada giggled. "Nothing will!" She turned to Ezomo. "You agree with the plan?"

Ezomo opened his mouth to speak, but before words could congregate on his tongue, something unexpected occurred.

The day before, the villagers had lodged a complaint

against the sun for sleeping too much and to redeem himself, the sun woke up extra early. As Ezomo started to answer Ada's question, a magnificent bright light hit the tops of the coconut trees and glanced off the anthills and shone on his face.

"The sun is awake!" Muja yelled.

Chimama gasped. "We got to get home before they find out we're gone!"

Chimama and Muja sprinted for the kapok tree.

Ezomo turned to follow them, but Ada gripped his arm. "Don't leave! Please! We need to find the leopard," she begged.

Ezomo pulled his arm away and ran after his friends.

It was Muja who first tried to climb up the slide, but the surface was too smooth, and he slid right back down. "Too slippery!" he yelled.

"How we get up?" Chimama asked frantically.

Ada appeared with Humongous perched on her shoulder.

"We must leave now!" Chimama yelled, shuffling her feet in the dirt.

"Calm down!" Muja yelled back. "I can't think."

Ezomo turned to Ada. "What should we do?"

Ada spoke quickly. "Let me take you behind the door to find the leopard."

"Nobody knows we're here. If we run home now, they will only fault us for going out at night. They will forgive us," Chimama said.

"Like they forgave me?" Ada snarled. "Don't you understand?"

"Understand what?" Muja yelled.

"You have passed the center point!"

"The what?" Chimama looked at Ezomo in alarm.

"Stupid children. It's the point where if you turn back, everything will remain the same. Like when Bisa begged me not to open the village door. Had I turned around and gone home, my life would have remained the same. Once you pass the center point, you change your destiny, and your life will *never* be the same."

"Can you ever return to your old life after the thenter point?" Chimama said with tears in her eyes.

"It's nearly impossible. But the three of you can!" said Ada.

"How?" Muja asked.

"We'll go behind the door, capture the leopard, and bring

it back. Then you will tell the Elders that the leopard stole you at night—walked right into your huts and grabbed you. But you managed to capture it. They will call you heroes. They will forgive you. Then you can return to your old lives, only better, because your mother will be able to cook, your father will be able to speak, and your dying mother will live. Why not let me take you behind the door huh?" Ada said.

"But can't we return to our old life without going behind the door?" Chimama asked.

"She can't keep answering your senseless questions!" Humongous said sharply.

"Where is the moon?" Ezomo asked suddenly, his voice cracking. "Where is it?" He turned swiftly in all directions, looking up bewildered at the sky. "Mamie!" He dropped on his knees and began to sob. His cry echoed across the Valley. It was the most sorrowful sound the forsaken people had ever heard.

18
De Children Are Missing

Back in Sesa, the villagers were vexed because the sun had woken them up before daybreak. They had lodged a complaint against the sun, but this was not the solution they had expected. Even the rooster was confused. It couldn't decide whether to crow or go back to sleep.

In Noroad, Muja's father decided to take his morning bath even though technically, it was still the middle of the night. He stretched his hand to Muja's mat and shook his son, but the shape under the brown cloth felt hard and not at all like Muja. Toba jerked his hand back and sat up straight. He rubbed his eyes. Slowly, he poked the cloth. He yanked the cloth away, and underneath it was a bag of rice. He lurched to his feet and gawked at it. Then he gently covered the rice again, as if covering Muja, and left the hut.

Outside, the sun shone wickedly and burned away the cool night air. Toba sat down on the ground. The lines on his forehead were scrunched, and he kept rubbing the sides of his face. Most of the residents of Noroad were outside of their shacks, too. Some stood fanning themselves with palm leaves and quarreling about the sun. Some sat looking hopeless. And some carried on with their usual morning routine, preparing maize porridge for breakfast, gathering dirty clothes to take to the river for washing, and attending to the children.

Toba scanned the crowd for Chimama's mother, Chima. If Muja went anywhere in the middle of the night, he thought, it would have to be to Chima's shack with his best friend, Chimama. He stood to go find Chima, but as soon as he did, he spotted her walking hurriedly toward him. She had both hands on her hips, and there was a line of women trailing her.

"Is Chimama with you?" Chima yelled across the compound.

Toba tapped his ear three times.

"I say is Chimama here? We can't find her-o."

Toba placed both hands on top of his head. Then he ran to Chima and grabbed her wrist. Pulling her inside of his hut, he showed her the bag of rice on Muja's mat.

"You mean Muja is gone too?" Chima shouted.

Toba nodded.

Chima ran out of the shack. "Muja and Chimama are missing!"

"You looked in the bush?" asked a man named Abe, pointing to the wooded area behind the compound.

"Yes. They not there," Chima said.

"You check the river?" a young boy named Omutu asked. "Maybe they went swimming."

Chima shook her head. "We just came from de river. They not there."

"But it's the middle of the night. They should be in their huts sleeping," Abe said. "Last time a child went missing in the middle of the night, our village door opened up, and something evil happened."

"We must alert the Elders!" someone shouted.

Chima, Toba, and the others scurried out of Noroad toward the compound where the Elders lived. As they hurried through Passtru the hunters, farmers, and fishers became alarmed when they heard the story of the missing children, so they followed the crowd. By the time Chima and Toba reached the Elders, almost the entire population of Sesa was with them.

After hearing the news, the Elders instructed the villagers to split up and search for Muja and Chimama. The load carriers, wood-carvers, and basket makers were ordered to search the market square. The farmers and fishers were ordered to search the farm and the areas near the river. The hunters were ordered to search the forest.

"Yesterday, that useless Ezomo was talking about the leopard that killed his father. He probably has something to do with this," one of the hunters said.

So someone was ordered to check Ezomo's hut to make sure he was there. They all agreed to meet under the Palaver Hut midmorning to report their findings.

19
To the Door

"**HOW** far is it if we take your way?" Ezomo asked. He and Chimama and Muja had finally agreed to go to the door with Ada. After all, it wasn't as though they really had a choice.

"About twenty thousand children steps," said Humongous with a sneer.

Muja swung the hunting bag over his shoulder. "We better get going then!"

"Follow me!" Ada yelled. She led Ezomo, Chimama, and Muja behind her dwelling to a spot where the land sloped downward and deepened into a narrow passageway with jagged boulders on both sides.

"A river is over there," Ada said, pointing to the far

end of the gully. "We'll take a boat to the forest." She hurried ahead. Ezomo, Chimama, and Muja followed her, Humongous hovering above their heads.

"It's really dark eh?" Chimama whispered. For although the sun was up early, it hadn't reached this deep spot.

Ezomo stretched his arms to the sides and felt for the giant rocks. He used them for balance as he edged forward. Muja had his fist clenched in front of his face, ready to punch anything that might jump out at him from the shadows.

"Over here!" Ada said, pressing her back against the wall to reveal a small eye of light peering at them from the end of the dark walkway. "That's where the river is."

Ezomo, Muja, and Chimama hurried after Ada.

Waiting for them at the end of the passageway was a narrow river with murky water and bulbine plants growing along it. Resting on the sandy riverbank was a canoe with two warped paddles inside. A piece of twine was tied to a cleat on the front of the boat, and the other end of the rope was tied to a bamboo stick jammed in the ground.

Ezomo scratched his head. "I don't understand. Why don't the forsaken people escape?"

Ada shrugged. "Escape to what? None of us are welcome

back in Sesa. Where will we go if we escape?" She twisted her mouth. "Come on! We must hurry."

Chimama stepped in first. Rainwater in the bottom of the canoe covered her feet and ankles.

Ada extended her hand to Ezomo. "Help me in, my friend," she said, throwing her rattan stick in the boat.

Ezomo didn't move. He looked at Muja.

"You grab that arm, and I'll grab this one," Muja said and placed Ada's left arm over his shoulders. Together, Ezomo and Muja helped Ada into the canoe where she sat in the puddle of water. "Stay here and look after Ofasa," she said to Humongous.

After Ezomo and Muja had stepped in the boat, Humongous used his beak to untie the line that kept the boat secured to the bank. "Off you go frisky impalas! Don't come back without that leopard!"

By the time the sun was actually supposed to rise, Ezomo, Muja, Chimama, and Ada had reached the forest. They were welcomed by chirping crickets and cackling tree frogs. Before them were the kapok trees with wide branches that towered over the wildflowers and evergreen plants growing on the forest floor. The air, hot and moist, carried the rotten scent of a dead bullfrog floating near the bank. Muja and Ezomo stepped carefully out of the canoe and into shallow waters. Their feet brushed against thick algae and slimy moss. Above them, the calls of crows resounded in the sky.

Together, the boys hauled the canoe to the grassy bank and anchored it to a stump. Chimama stepped out into thick grass that reached her knees. She swatted fat mosquitos biting her arms and legs as she waited for Ezomo and Muja to help Ada out of the canoe.

"Over there is the way to the door," Ada said, pointing with her rattan stick. With the back of her thumb, she wiped sweat from her forehead and hobbled into the mass of trees. Ezomo, Muja, and Chimama followed.

"Never been to this part of the forest before," Muja said.

Ezomo stayed close to Ada. Images of Yatta lying on the ground in their hut flashed through his mind. What if Ada's lying, he thought. He glanced at Ada, who had stopped to gawk at a monkey hanging upside down in a banana tree. Something was suspicious about her eyes. He wasn't sure he trusted her.

"Why did you want us to come see you at night?" Ezomo asked her.

Without taking her eyes off the monkey, Ada said, "What are you talking about?"

"You told Humongous that you would only see us at night. Why?"

Ada sighed deeply. "At night, there are no hunters in the forest."

Ezomo scratched the top of his head. "It was rest day when we came to see you. The hunters were not in the forest."

"I forgot." Ada shrugged. "All of the days are the same in the Valley."

"How do you know the leopard has magic powers?" asked Ezomo.

Ada fidgeted with the kola nut around her neck. "I saw it doing magic. Didn't you see it too?"

"What did you see—"

"A-hey! Found them!"

Ezomo was interrupted by a familiar voice. He looked up.

Ada ducked behind the banana tree.

"Bisa!" Ezomo exclaimed.

The bird landed on a branch and folded his wings. "E are in big, big trouble! Where e going?"

"To the village door," Chimama said without thinking. "The leopard witching our parent is behind it."

Bisa gasped. "Have e lost all your senses?" He shook his head gravely. "E have done a terrible thing. When I tell the Elders, they will surely ban e children from the village."

Muja rushed to Bisa. "The leopard brought us here! It stole us from our huts."

Bisa soared off, still scolding.

"Chimama, why did you say that!" said Muja.

"We are in big trouble now," said Ezomo, his face scrunched with fear.

"I didn't mean—" Chimama was interrupted by Ada.

"We must hurry now," Ada said, emerging from her hiding spot. "Follow me!"

They walked as fast as they could, parting thick branches, scrambling up rocky slopes and down small hills. Their clothes were wet from sweat, and their mouths dry from thirst.

"I think Ada is lying," Ezomo whispered to Muja.

"She's not!" Muja said firmly. "But one of us must carry her. We'll never make it at this pace."

Chimama placed both hands on her hips. "Good idea, you do it."

Muja sighed. He turned to Ada. "Get on my back." He crouched low and once her arms were fastened around his neck, he continued on again.

Ada directed them through the thick shrubs. Their legs trampled wild vines while their hands parted twisty branches.

"That way!" Ada yelled, pointing to a narrow dirt path just visible in the thick vegetation.

Muja ran down the path as fast as he could with the extra weight on his back. Ezomo and Chimama followed close behind him.

"*Shhh* . . . I hear thomething," Chimama hissed.

They all froze. They heard faint voices shouting in the distance.

Ezomo leaned close to Muja and Chimama. "But what if Ada *is* lying?" he whispered.

"Hurry!" Ada yelled from Muja's back. "Faster!"

Chimama bowed her head and spoke quietly. "Why would Ada lie?"

Ezomo shrugged. "Don't know." The voices were getting

so close that Ezomo could practically make out the words. "We must hurry!" he said.

Ada kicked Muja's hip with her heel. "You're slow as an old goat. Move it! "

Ezomo, Muja, and Chimama sprinted on under the canopy of branches.

"There!" Ada announced, pointing to the wooden door covered in green moss. She smiled broadly and slid off Muja's back.

The voices drew nearer.

Ada pushed Ezomo toward the door. "Quick! Open it!"

Ezomo swallowed hard. "Me?"

"No the sky! Of course you. Go!" She stared at him with wide eyes, like an owl watching the night. He raised his hand and reached slowly toward the door. His fingertips brushed against the moss.

"Quick!" Ada yelled. Her voice reverberated through the trees. "Now!" she snarled, slamming her stick against the door.

Ezomo gripped the thick knob. It felt slimy, like the back of a wet frog. He inhaled deeply and closed his eyes. Then he pushed. To his surprise, the door didn't open—not even a crack. He pressed his palms against it and pushed again.

He looked at Muja and then at Ada. "It won't open!"

Muja slammed his body against it. The door remained closed. He knelt and yanked the bottom of it. The door shook but stayed shut. He kicked it twice.

Muja looked at Ada. "What we do now?" he said, panting.

"Worthless children!" Ada leapt forward and whacked the door with her cane. But nothing happened.

"Maybe we have to break it," Muja said.

"Great idea!" Ada said, spinning around.

"Over there!" Chimama said, pointing to a big rock resting underneath a tree. "We can use that."

Muja, Chimama, and Ezomo rushed to the rock. Together, they lifted and carried it to the door.

"Hit the edge," Ezomo said, gasping for breath.

They thrust the rock against the side of the door. The door sprung slightly ajar.

Ada grinned. "Follow me!"

Chimama was the first to slide her body through the narrow opening behind Ada. Next was Muja, and he went through as easily as Chimama had. Ezomo thought his heart would jump out of his chest as the voices of the villagers drew nearer and nearer.

Just as he slid through, a group of hunters appeared at the far end of the dirt path, about fifty steps away from the door. They were holding spears. Behind them stood the Elders, holding their stools. Ezomo spotted Chima and Toba. Toba's eyes were red, and Chima's jaw hung with sorrow. He searched for his mother, forgetting briefly that she was lying on the dirt floor in their hut.

"It's the useless boy!" one of the hunters shouted.

"Come on!" Muja pulled his arm.

Ezomo looked over his shoulder and saw the hunters charging toward him. He squeezed his chest and head through the opening. His left arm followed. He heard a shriek and felt hands tugging his leg. Ezomo yanked his leg away and slid his entire body through. Behind him, the door slammed shut.

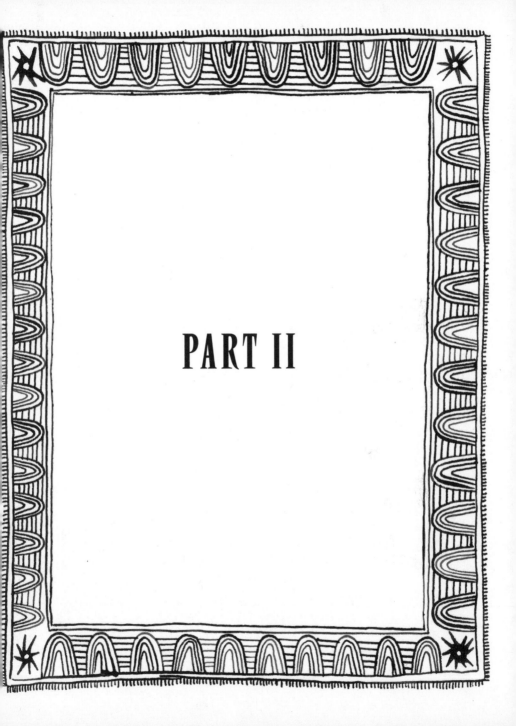

PART II

I

The Other Side

Behind the village door was a swamp that stretched far and kept going, becoming wider and wider, twisting and turning, going this way then that way, forgetting where it started and where it was meant to go.

Around the edge of the swamp grew fleshy water cabbage with leafy heads where mosquitos hid their eggs. Hippo grass and liverworts flourished in the stale water. Sprouting out of that same water were arching papyrus weeds with bushy crowns. It was on these that the black crake birds rested after filling their bellies with worms and tadpoles. The swamp hummed with plenty more creatures. Bullfrogs splashed in sour water. Lizards slithered on mats of hairy moss. Grasshoppers darted through prickly grass.

For years the swamp had been left alone, having only been disturbed once by a bright-eyed child, once by a cantankerous kingfisher bird, and once by a creature that passed too quickly for the swamp to decipher who or what it was. But on this day, the village door sprung open and out stumbled four children.

Their names were Ezomo, Chimama, Muja, and Ada. They had come from the village of Sesa. They had come to find a leopard. This is what was whispered among the frogs and lizards and grasshoppers and mosquitos. This news spread wide and deep until it reached the ears of the swamp. The swamp shrieked and creaked, then stretched her back to make space for the children.

Ezomo's eyes traveled across the swamp, seeing quickly what they needed to see. The swamp, Ezomo thought, was frightful in feeling and appearance. He was sure evil spirits dwelled there. And crocodiles. His eyes, jumping from here to there, saw that the swamp offered him no comfort. His rock wasn't there, and neither were the long stretches of road where he idled in sorrow. Worst, the swamp offered him no promise of saving his mother. He felt the knot in his belly tighten. He needed to sit with his knot, for there was no other way to loosen it. He needed to be brave. He needed to find the leopard and hurry home before the moon grew full.

"What now?" Ezomo asked, his voice trembling. He looked at where Ada was supposed to be, only she wasn't. "Ada?"

"Where did Ada go eh?" Chimama said, her face pale.

"She . . . she . . . she was just here." Muja spun around.

Between the small time they had opened the door and that moment, Ada had vanished.

Ezomo felt his heart drop. The lie he had seen in Ada's eyes was now the truth coming to pass. He turned and looked at the village door. Behind it was a home he could no longer return to. Not without the leopard. In front of him was a place he didn't know, a place cold and frightful. Something else was troubling him. The sun, having been quarreled at for waking too early, was already beginning to set, and nighttime was rising. They had lost one whole day.

"We must find the leopard soon," Ezomo urged.

"But how?" Chimama asked. "How will we find the leopard without Ada?"

Ezomo kept quiet for his mouth was full of doubt. Ada's words played in his head. They were quick and nimble those words of hers, slipping past truth and lingering in lies. She had, in fact, spoken very little about the leopard. She had evaded big questions and had confronted only small ones. And yet, they had been so quick to follow her. They had been like lambs following a fox to its den. Ezomo felt the knot in his stomach grow.

"Don't know where Ada went," Muja said. "But we must find—"

"Ada lied!" Ezomo cried out. "I saw it in her eyes when she spoke about the leopard!"

Muja recoiled. "Why didn't you say something?"

"I did!"

"No, you didn't!" said Muja.

"In the forest. I told you," argued Ezomo.

Muja paused to think. He shook his head. "What would she gain by lying?"

"Coming here was bad," Chimama whimpered. "Evil thpirits live here." Her lips trembled. "This is all your fault Muja."

"Me! How?"

"You told us you had a plan! We followed you."

"You said you were tired of seeing shame in your mother's eyes." Muja looked down. "You said you wanted to sit in the middle row under the mango tree, next to the other girls, and feel like a treasure instead of a castaway."

"Forget what I said," Chimama whispered. "Let's go back!"

"We can't," Muja sputtered. "Not without the leopard."

"Muja's right," Ezomo said somberly. "If we return without the leopard, they will send us to the Valley."

Chimama covered her face and began to cry. "We won't find the leopard without Ada. Opening the door was a bad idea. Evil thpirit live here!" She glanced at the sky. "And the night is coming fast. What will we do?"

"Don't cry, Chimama," Ezomo said, edging closer to her.

"Yes, don't cry." Muja tapped the hunting bag around his waist. "We will catch the leopard and go home. They will call us heroes."

Chimama dried her eyes and nodded.

Ezomo nodded too. Then he and Chimama followed Muja into the swamp.

2

The Leopard Behind the Moon

The crake birds watched Ezomo, Chimama, and Muja creeping away from the village door, stepping carefully on the mats of soggy moss growing along the edge of the swamp. Their feet dragged. Their mouths sagged. The courage of yesterday had left them, and worry had taken its place.

"Over there!" whispered Muja, pointing to a colony of cattails. "Something's moving."

He was right. Something shuffled between the grass.

The children crept forward. Muja clutched the net he'd yanked from the hunting bag. Chimama bit her tongue. Ezomo held his breath.

"What if it hurts us eh?" Chimama whispered.

"*Shhh . . .*"

Sensing the children approaching, the thing in the cat-tails lunged, revealing itself to be a turtle, not a leopard. It scuttled away.

Panic rushed to Ezomo's chest. "Ada lied!"

Muja didn't respond. He'd stepped over a rotten log and ducked under a canopy of woody vines, venturing deeper into the swamp. Ezomo and Chimama followed him, their feet sinking in mud, their muscles tight with fear.

"Why would Ada bring us here for nothing?" Chimama said. "Ada is good."

"How do you know?" Ezomo asked.

"She gave us water to drink and took us to the door."

"Humpf," said Ezomo.

Muja stood in a small clearing, straining his neck to see far into the swamp, to see what more was there. "We must find somewhere safe to sleep before the night arrives," he said.

"How about near the village door?" Chimama suggested.

"Not a good idea."

"Why not?"

"We'll be going backward. We need to go forward."

"I want to be near the door."

"No."

"Yeth."

"No Chimama."

"Yeth!"

As Muja and Chimama quarreled over where to sleep, Ezomo kept his eyes on the sky, where something strange was happening. The moon had appeared, different than before. It was now deep yellow, orange almost, and its dark splotches had separated into smaller pieces. Moreover, it had eaten more light from the sun and was growing full.

Ezomo's mouth fell open. "Oh!" He pointed to the moon. Chimama and Muja looked up.

"What happened to the moon?" Muja said. "It looks . . . it looks . . . it looks like—"

"A leopard," Ezomo said.

"Oh . . ." Chimama's eyes were wide.

Indeed, the moon resembled a leopard—an orange one with black spots.

"It moved!" Ezomo looked at Chimama and Muja. "Did you see it? It moved! The moon. It moved!" He rubbed his eyes. Yatta had told him that the moon was a mother watching over her sleeping children. When evil happened at night, it was because the moon had fallen asleep. And whenever the moon appeared to be gone, it was only hiding, watching to see if her children behaved in her absence. But what hovered before him now in the night sky was no mother moon, Ezomo thought. It was something else.

"The leopard . . ." Ezomo paused and waited for the right words to gather on his tongue. "The leopard is . . ." More words arrived. "The leopard is behind the moon!"

Muja frowned. "How . . . how . . . how can the leopard be behind the moon? How would it even get there?"

"Witchcraft!" Chimama yelled, scaring the lizards listening in the bush.

"It moved again!" Ezomo said, hands on top of his head. "I saw it!"

Indeed, the moon had shifted slightly in the sky.

"I saw it too!" Muja said. "The leopard is definitely hiding behind the moon!"

"What do we do?" Ezomo asked Muja.

Muja looked to his left and then to his right. The answer he sought was not in the swamp. He looked at the sky, at the moon inching across it. "We follow it," he said and started to run.

☒ ☒ ☒

The crake birds scattered as Muja, Ezomo, and Chimama hurried past. They whispered to one another that the children were chasing the moon because a leopard was hiding behind it. The lizards, hearing the news, whispered among themselves that the children were stupid for believing that a leopard could hide behind a moon. Leopards were cunning, but they could not travel to the moon. The crake birds, hearing the words of the lizards, said it was the lizards who were stupid, not the children, for if lizards could fly, they would see that in the sky was indeed a moon that resembled a leopard.

The night took no notice. It grew darker and darker and gathered up all the sounds left behind by the day, and all the warmth too, leaving only a cool stillness.

Finally, Muja stopped running. "It's not moving any-more," he said, pointing to the moon.

"What we do now eh?" Chimama asked.

"We wait. We wait until it moves again," Muja said.

And that is just what they did. They sat and waited, watching the sky.

Ezomo thought about Yatta and wondered if she was

alone in their hut. Had anyone fed her? He sighed. He was hungry too, but now was not the time to think of food. Feeling weary, he laid his head on the skin of the swamp. Nearby, he heard Chimama's slow breathing. Muja was muttering words he couldn't understand.

They waited and waited. And waited. But unfortunately, their eyes were tired and their sleep impatient, for it had been a long journey from Noroad to the Valley, and from the Valley to the forest, then through the village door and now the swamp. And so, one by one, they fell asleep. The swamp curled, softening her moss, and let the children rest.

3
One Last Thing

The next day, before the sun came to collect the morning dew, Ezomo woke up. He lay staring at the sour water, at the mosquitos buzzing over fleshy cabbage, and thought himself to be inside a dream. Squeezing his eyes closed, he tried to wake himself, and when the memory of opening the village door crossed his mind, he jumped up.

Chimama was curled up next to him, her arms folded under her head. Muja was beside her, his arms and legs sprawled over the moss.

"Wake up!" Ezomo said, yanking Chimama's arm. "Muja! Wake up!"

Chimama sat up and shivered. She yawned loudly. Then she stretched her eyes wide and jumped up. "Eh! Where are we?"

"The swamp," Ezomo said. "The swamp behind the village door."

Chimama frowned. "Did we catch the leopard?"

Ezomo shook his head. "Not yet." He took a deep breath. "Only one day left."

"One day left for what?"

"Before Mamie dies. The moon will be full tomorrow night."

Chimama bowed her head.

"The leopard can't hide forever," Muja said, sitting up and rubbing his eyes. "It will have to come down soon to hunt, and when it does, we will catch it."

Ezomo nodded, but in his heart, he felt great doubt. What if the leopard was leading them to danger? Worse, what if the leopard was leading them nowhere. Sending them in circles, so they found no beginning and also no end.

"We need to eat," Chimama announced.

Ezomo looked around. Daylight was budding. "We need to find the leopard."

"If I don't eat soon, I will die."

"You won't die," Muja said. He turned to Ezomo. "Don't worry. When the sun comes out, the moon will arrive to eat the sun's light. And if the leopard is hiding behind it, we will catch it." He placed his hand over his brow and scanned the area. "Now we must find food." He hugged his shoulders. "And we must make fire."

They decided that Ezomo and Chimama would hunt for food while Muja looked for wood to make fire.

"You think they're waiting for us at the door?" Chimama asked as she and Ezomo walked along the rim of the swamp.

"They're probably in the Palaver Hut, deciding our fate," Ezomo said.

"What you think happened to Ada?"

Ezomo shrugged.

"You think we're lost?"

"I don't know Chimama," said Ezomo, wishing he had answers for his friend.

When they gathered back together, Muja's arms overflowed with woody plants but Chimama's mouth hung low, for the only food she and Ezomo had managed to find was wild rice, which hadn't yet ripened.

"We can roast the rice," Ezomo said. "I've seen my mother do it."

"We need fire first," Muja said. Kneeling, he attempted

to make a fire, but after fumbling a good while, not a pinch of smoke appeared.

"You don't know how to make fire?" asked Chimama with wide eyes.

Muja didn't answer. He tried again, but it was in vain. The fire refused to start.

"All that big mouth, and you can't even make fire?" mocked Chimama. She covered her mouth with her lappa and laughed.

"I know how," Ezomo mumbled.

"You?" Chimama twisted her mouth. "If you can make fire, then my mother can cook."

"My father showed me. Before he died." Ezomo knelt beside Muja and pulled two sticks from the pile—one flat and one long and pointy. He pressed his knee on the flat stick and began scraping it with the tip of the pointy stick.

"Try your other hand too," Chimama suggested.

Ezomo wrapped his left palm over his right and scraped some more.

"This will help," Muja said, tossing grass on the wood.

Ezomo scraped until he was out of breath, and then he kept scraping, stopping only once to wipe sweat from his forehead. Back and forth, push and pull, he struggled on, and just as defeat began spreading across his face, Ezomo heard and saw something—a little flick, a subtle crackle, and smoke. He stretched his lips and blew small breeze to help the fire catch. Chimama rushed to throw more grass on the flame.

"I made fire," Ezomo said, his eyes glinting. He stepped back and observed the growing flame. It crackled and popped. "Wish my mother could see this."

Muja put his arm around Ezomo's shoulders. "Thought they said you were useless?"

Ezomo, Muja, and Chimama sat by the fire, roasting wild rice while waiting for the moon to appear. Around them, the day ripened, filling up with chirps and hums and snarls too. They traded stories and memories and lamented how different things would be if Toba could speak, and Chima could cook, and if Ezomo's father was alive and his mother well, and if they could sit in the middle row under the mango tree. When the morning left and the afternoon arrived, they became impatient. So they exchanged secrets and made promises. And told riddles. Once, and only briefly, they shared a laugh. Carrying on this way, they were able to tolerate the slow passing of the afternoon.

"What else did your father teach you?" Muja asked as they roasted and peeled wild nuts Chimama had shaken off a bush.

Ezomo felt the knot in his stomach harden. He wasn't accustomed to speaking about his father. Once, while Yatta fed him a bitter concoction to loosen his grief, he'd asked if his father was a brave warrior when he died, and Yatta— looking around anxiously—had said that his father wasn't actually part of the hunting contest. A great famine had arrived that year. Many animals and crops died. The Elders had ordered the bravest and strongest men in Sesa to hunt for meat, promising to reward the one who seized the most. His father, she whispered, was not among the men chosen. He had been merely waiting to tote the load of the hunters when the leopard attacked him. Ezomo saw embarrassment in her eyes, and from that day on, he'd thought of his father's death as a disgraceful thing to be spoken about only in whispers. His heart swelled with shame and guilt each time he longed to speak of his papa.

Chimama pointed to the sandy soil. "Draw him."

"Who?"

"Your father. Draw what you remember about him."

Ezomo swallowed. There wasn't much he remembered. All the memories he had savored were old and worn, and he wasn't sure which memories were real and which ones he improvised.

"Go on. Draw him," said Chimama.

Ezomo shifted onto his knees and hovered over the soil. He drew a round head with almond-shaped eyes, a nose resembling a cocoa bean, and a slanted line for a mouth. Then he drew a lean body with long arms and legs. He finished by drawing ears and some hair.

Chimama covered her mouth with the tail of her lappa and giggled. "What funny feet." She laughed some more. "I like your father's hair."

Ezomo studied the drawing. It looked nothing like the worn memories he kept in his mind.

"What was he like?" Muja asked.

Ezomo felt uneasy. The tightness rose from his belly to his chest. His mind chased a memory of sitting by the river with his father, and another of strolling with his father on the wide mud road. The crake birds fluttered past and whispered that the moon was finally coming. But Ezomo didn't hear them, for he was busy chasing old memories.

"We used to sit together by the river," Ezomo said. He frowned. "I just wanted to tell him one last thing before that leopard killed him."

Muja leaned close. "What did you want to tell him?"

Ezomo felt the tightening sensation rise to his throat. He pushed it down with a swallow, but when he opened his mouth to speak, the tightening rushed out as a wail.

Chimama placed her arms around Ezomo and held him while he wept. Muja held Ezomo's hand.

The tears flowed for a good while, and once they stopped, Ezomo lifted his head from Chimama's shoulder. He felt small peace.

"Look!" Chimama said, pointing to the sky.

Ezomo looked and saw that the moon had appeared. In the fading daylight, it looked pale, but he could still see the spots. He jumped up. "Let's follow it!"

"Quick! Put out the fire," Muja said, tossing mud on the flame.

The three of them rushed to put out the fire. Then, with Ezomo in the lead, they hurried after the moon.

4

Believe

Ezomo, Muja, and Chimama chased the moon through thick reeds higher than their heads and through water so boundless their feet barely reached the ground. Grasshoppers and mosquitos followed them. News traveled that the children were deep in the swamp and that they were still chasing the leopard. Hearing this news, the lizards said that the children were indeed stupid, for even if a leopard was hiding behind the moon, how did they intend to catch it from the swamp? The crake birds, overhearing the lizards, said the lizards were the stupid ones because the moon would eventually shrink, and when it did, the leopard would fall.

Ezomo stopped running. He had the same thought as the lizards. "How will we catch the leopard from down here?"

"With my net," Muja said, tapping his father's hunting bag.

"Your net can't reach the sky."

Muja scratched his head. "Maybe the leopard will get hungry and come down soon."

A sickening thought crossed Ezomo's mind. "What if it doesn't?"

"When the moon gets hot, the leopard will come down to cool off," Chimama reasoned. "It won't remain up there long."

"But what if it does?"

Muja gripped Ezomo's arm. "We must believe. We can't return to the village without the leopard. We must believe the leopard will come down."

Ezomo's mind drifted to a story he once heard Old Man Flomo tell about a dragonfly that caught a young mosquito. Just as Dragonfly opened his mouth to eat his catch, Mosquito begged Dragonfly to spare his life for a short while so he could see the sun. He wanted to see the glorious light the older mosquitos talked so much about. Dragonfly agreed to spare Mosquito's life for one night so that Mosquito could see the sunrise in the morning. So Mosquito sat by the river and waited all night for the sun to rise. Finally, in the early morning, just as the sun was about to come up, Dragonfly had a change of heart. He decided he was too hungry to wait and was going to eat Mosquito for breakfast. "Don't eat me please," Mosquito begged. "I haven't seen the sun." Dragonfly approached Mosquito anyhow with a wide mouth. "If you eat me, you will turn into stone!" Mosquito shouted. Dragonfly wasn't deterred. His belly rumbled. He wanted food. Mosquito squeezed his eyes shut as Dragonfly placed him in his mouth and swallowed. When Mosquito opened his eyes again, he thought he would find himself in Dragonfly's dark belly, but instead, he was sitting on a stone. Mosquito looked at the stone and yelled, "Told you!" He had believed so strongly that Dragonfly would turn into a stone if it ate him that it had actually happened.

"Maybe rain will push the leopard out of the moon," Ezomo said.

Muja nodded. "Yes, that's possible."

Ezomo gawked at the sky. It was clear with no sign of rain. He inhaled the sour air and let it out his mouth and dashed after the moon.

☒ ☒ ☒

They ran and ran and ran some more. They ran past a soggy lagoon and past a tiny island teeming with vines. Past an area with knobby trees growing in green water and still the spotted moon was before them. Then the swamp narrowed, becoming smaller and smaller, its water sinking lower and lower until it found its beginning, and there was where it ended.

"Look!" Muja said, pointing to dry land in the distance.

"Food!" Chimama said.

Ezomo gazed ahead. Before him was the end of the swamp, and beyond that a sugarcane farm, and beyond that, he saw a village.

5

Celebration of the Tree

Ezomo, Chimama, and Muja climbed out of the swamp and stood on the bank. Before them were rows and rows of leafy green sugarcane. Some stalks stood tall and strong, having already matured. Other plants stood limp in the soil, their maturity still ripening. The friends gaped at the farm, inhaling the sour air, wondering where they were. Around them, the day, having lost its youth, was fading into evening.

"The leopard is going to that village," Ezomo said, pointing to the moon drifting across the sky.

"Let's follow it!" Muja said. "The villagers will help us catch it."

Chimama said nothing. She was busy gnawing a sugarcane stalk.

Between the rows of leafy sugarcane was a crooked path paved with small rocks. It was on this path that Ezomo, Chimama, and Muja traveled, passing a field of cassava and a field of sweet potatoes before finally reaching a creek that separated the farm from the village. They heard the sounds of village life: water being drawn from a well, chickens clucking, goats bleating, and children playing. Somewhere, someone was chopping wood.

Across the creek, grapefruit, butter pear, and papaya trees sprawled over a green field. At the far edge of the field, a row of thorny wait-a-bit bushes protected the village. Over the tops of the bushes, they could see giant houses with red roofs standing in the shade of coconut trees.

"They have plenty crops here," Chimama said, pointing to the fruit trees.

"Do you see the size of the houses?" asked Muja. "They're so big."

Ezomo gazed at the village, at the narrowing sunlight flickering on the roofs. Facing his back was the farm and behind it, the swamp. And somewhere inside the swamp was the village door. Oma said evil spirits lived behind the door, but he hadn't seen any in the swamp or any on the farm. What about the village? Did it hold the evil Oma spoke of under the mango tree?

"Think it's safe to go there?" Ezomo asked.

Muja frowned. "Why wouldn't it be?"

Ezomo looked around. "I have a funny feeling."

"What feeling?" Chimama said.

"In my stomach. I don't know." He glanced at the thorny bushes, at the grand houses. "Why would the leopard come here?"

Muja pointed to the bushes. "We'll hide there and wait. And when we see that the village is safe, we'll go and tell the people about the leopard. They will help us catch it."

With a plan in place, Ezomo, Chimama, and Muja waded across the creek and crept between the fruit trees. They ducked behind a wait-a-bit bush and sent their eyes to investigate the village.

What their eyes saw was a village square surrounded by grand houses and bitter leaf trees. Sitting on a stool in the center of the square was a small boy with the ways of a big man. He sat with his chest puffed, this boy-man, bobbing his bald head as he ate from a bowl resting on his lap. Between each grab of food, he pounded his fist on the ground, drummed his chest like one preparing to fight, and clutched a necklace made of leaves dangling around his neck. Now and then, his mouth opened wide, and out of it spilled a wicked laugh that made the stray chickens shriek and scatter.

A few paces in front of the boy sat a group of men, women, and children, all wearing red, free-flowing robes with elaborate prints and patterns. They sat eating rice and meat, their backs stiff with pride, their chins high as if there was a faraway place they were all trying to see. None of them had any hair. Behind them sat a larger group of men, women, and children, all bald and all wearing yellow robes and all stuffing their mouths with food, laughing and chatting gleefully. Among them were boys and girls holding drums and shekeres. Sitting at the very back of the crowd, behind the men and women wearing yellow robes, was a smaller group of villagers, wearing dingy lappas and wrappers, their eyes filled with a longing too deep for anyone to reach. They sat quietly, like small children in trouble, eating and straining their necks to see the boy on the stool.

There was something else. A tree, right behind the boy. It stood around five feet tall with a trunk as black as night.

Its roots grew above the soil rather than under, and its limbs grew down rather than up. Three crooked branches sprouted out of the trunk and on each dangled a few yellow leaves.

"What a strange tree," whispered Ezomo.

"What's strange is that none of these people have any hair!" said Muja.

"*Shhhh,*" hissed Chimama.

Ezomo fidgeted in his hiding place behind the bush. The village with its grand houses, bald citizens, and strange tree had stirred the sour feeling in his stomach. They needed to catch the leopard soon and hurry home.

"Who's that?" Muja whispered.

A man with a lanky frame and a small head marched to the center of the square and stood beside the boy. In his hand he held a hunting horn, and once he blew it, the villagers ceased eating and talking and directed their eyes to him.

"Probably the village orator," Ezomo said.

Chimama pressed her fingers against her lips. "Be quiet."

"We shall begin!" the man announced.

The villagers rose and cheered.

Ezomo frowned. "They're having some kind of ceremony."

"For what?" asked Muja.

"If you're quiet, we will know," Chimama said.

"Is today not an important day for the people of Ekewe?" the orator began.

"Indeed!" the villagers shouted.

"And is it not today that we waited for all day yesterday?"

"Indeed!"

"And is it not today that Yeanue will continue protecting our tree?"

"Indeed!"

"And is it not time for us to start the celebration of our village tree?"

"Indeed!"

Boys slammed their palms on drums. Girls shook shekeres. Men, women, and children sprang to their feet and danced. The boy on the stool laughed, then quickly sat down and resumed eating, a grin on his face.

As Ezomo watched the villagers dance, a great panic budded in his chest. If these villagers were anything like the people of Sesa, the ceremony would last way into the night, and by the time it ended, the moon would be gone. His thoughts fed his panic, so much so that the panic grew big and swallowed Ezomo, and with Ezomo in its mouth, it stood and spoke on his behalf: "We can't just wait behind this bush! My mother is dying!"

"*Shhhh!*" Muja shushed his friend. "What do you suggest we do?"

"We have to tell them about the leopard. We have to tell them now!"

Chimama looked at her friends. "What about that strange—"

Ezomo cut her off. "We'll go and ask for their help. If something evil happens, we'll run back to the farm."

"What a stupid plan!" Muja said.

"Why?" asked Ezomo.

"Because Chimama runs like a turtle."

"I do not!"

"You do. If we run, they will catch you *and* Ezomo."

Meanwhile, as Ezomo, Muja, and Chimama argued, the boy sitting on the stool stopped eating. His eyes, thinking they saw something moving behind the bushes at the edge of the square, focused to see what was there. A child they had never seen before rose from behind a bush. The eyes grew suspicious, and as they inspected the child, two more children rose from behind the bush, and after inspecting them too, the eyes quickly deduced that these three children did not belong to the village of Ekewe. It was then that the eyes returned to the boy and after showing the boy what they saw, the boy jumped up and yelled, "Thieves in our village! Thieves!"

But the villagers did not hear the boy shouting over the drums and the shekeres, so they carried on with the celebration.

Ezomo, Chimama, and Muja, who had not heard the boy yell either, were still arguing about what to do.

"I'll go talk to the villagers while you two wait here," Muja suggested. "If I detect something strange, I'll scratch my chin." He scratched his chin to show them how he would do it. "If you see me scratch, run back to the farm and hide. I will catch up with you."

Worry settled on Ezomo's face. "That's not a good plan."

"Why not?"

"What if they catch you?"

"I'll be fine."

"No!" Chimama said. "We can't leave anyone behind."

Ezomo bit his lip. "What if we take—"

No one will ever know what Ezomo intended to say because before more words could leave his mouth, the horn blew again, and silence fell like rain during raining season.

"Over there!" Ezomo heard someone shout. Turning, he saw the boy in the square, standing and pointing the horn at him.

"Thieves! They have come to steal leaves from our tree!" the boy yelled, charging toward Ezomo, Muja, and Chimama, like a wild pig charging a sheep. The villagers raced behind him, shoving and shouting, unsure where they were headed or who they were after.

Ezomo, Chimama, and Muja froze. Their feet attached to the ground like roots on an old tree.

The boy skidded to a stop in front of Ezomo. "Thieves!"

"We're not!" Chimama shouted back, hands on her hips.

The boy frowned. Up close, his face was very round and very shiny and it sat atop a very broad body with very thick arms and very stubby legs. A short giant, he appeared to be, and yet his eyes were soft, like those belonging to a young impala.

"Where you na come from?" the boy said, legs apart and hands on his hips.

"Sesa," Muja said, standing tall. "We're from the village of Sesa."

The boy's eyes wandered from Muja's head down to Muja's feet. Then those eyes jumped over to Ezomo, and after inspecting him too, crossed over to Chimama where they stayed only briefly before returning to Muja. "Liar! You na come to steal leaves from our tree!"

"No. We didn't," Ezomo said, shaking his head. "We came to catch the leopard."

Some of the villagers gasped.

The boy turned to Ezomo. "What leopard?"

Ezomo pointed up. "The leopard hiding behind the moon."

The villagers, who crowded in a great mob behind the boy, gawked at the sky. The boy gawked too, his eyes darting around until they found the pale moon. "Liar! There's no leopard behind the moon!"

But Ezomo didn't hear him, for he too was looking at the moon which was now gray and without spots. The leopard was gone. "Where did it go?" he said, turning to Muja and Chimama.

"It fell!" Muja said, his eyes wide. He looked in the thorn bushes behind him. "It's around here!" He turned to the villagers. "Please! Help us find it."

"Quiet!" the boy yelled. "You think we're fools?"

The villagers murmured. A few of them jeered. "They think we're fools!"

"The leopard fell," Ezomo tried to explain. "We must find it! The moon will—"

"I said silence!" Froth slipped out of the boy's mouth and sat on his bottom lip. "There's no leopard here! You na come steal from our tree. Thieves! Liars!"

"Thieves!" the villagers chanted. "Liars!"

The panic in Ezomo swelled, causing him to sway, lose his balance, and fall.

Chimama rushed to kneel beside him. "Are you all right?"

Ezomo didn't answer. He was back in Sesa, in his mind, that is. He was on the gravel path, running to his hut, and arriving there, he hurried inside and sat beside Yatta, and whispered that he was sorry he couldn't save her, because after all his efforts, he was still just a useless boy.

"Get up!" the boy shouted at Ezomo.

"Leave him alone!" yelled Muja, his jaw clenched.

The boy drew phlegm from his throat, spat it on the ground, and thumped his chest. "You na challenge me!" His eyes turned red. "You na come steal from our tree, and now you na challenge me to fight!"

"No! We came to find the leopard. We came to save Ezomo's mother. She's going to die. He already has no father." Tears clung to the lids of Muja's eyes. "We came because Chimama's mother can't cook. She's the only woman in our village who can't even boil rice. Do you know how shameful that is?" The tears shook. "And we came because my father lost his voice. He was the greatest hunter in Sesa. Now he can't even speak." The tears lost their grip and fell.

"Lizard tears!" the boy mocked. "I don't believe you!"

"We don't believe you!" chanted the crowd.

"I'm telling the truth!" Muja said, his voice jittering. "My father used to speak, and now he doesn't. No one respects him or me." He cupped his face and began to weep.

The tightness in the boy's face loosened. His glare lost its fire. His fists unfolded. "Why your father can't speak?"

Muja uncovered his face. He wiped his eyes with his arm.

"No one knows. One morning, he woke up, and his voice was just gone."

The villagers began to murmur. The boy glanced over his shoulders at them, gesturing for silence, then turned his attention back to Muja. "When that happened? When he na stop speaking?"

"Two years ago."

More murmuring filled the air.

"So your father used to talk?"

The crowd, silent now, waited to hear Muja's response.

The only sound was from a bird cracking a nut.

"Yes."

"Then one day he lost his voice?"

"Yes."

"Just like that?"

"Yes."

The villagers erupted in loud chatter, causing such a commotion that the orator had to blow the horn to silence them.

"We think the leopard is to blame for all of it," Chimama said once the crowd settled down again. "We think the leopard is witching our parents."

"What's your name?" asked the boy. His voice was quick and quarrelsome.

"Chimama."

He nodded at Muja. "You?"

"I'm Muja."

"What about him?" the boy said, pointing to Ezomo.

"My name is Ezomo," Ezomo said and stood.

"I'm Yeanue." The boy raised his chin. "I'm the village tree protector."

Ezomo had never heard of such a thing. "What's that?" he asked.

Yeanue looked at Ezomo indignantly. "Plenty people na try stealing leaves."

"Why would people want to steal leaves from a tree?" asked Muja.

"Because they're thieves! Like you!" Yeanue sucked his teeth. "Our village tree was here before my father and mother na born. Long ago, when the tree . . ."

But Ezomo had stopped listening. Yeanue's tongue held too many words, and there wasn't enough time for his ears to hear them all. He didn't want to talk about the tree. He wanted to talk about the leopard. He wanted to ask the villagers to help him catch it, but he was afraid that if he did, the boy would shout "Liar!" and "Thief!" and these people might seize him and Muja and Chimama and tie them up, and then he would never make it home. Maybe if they left now without causing trouble, he could make it back in time to say goodbye to his mother. "We have to go," Ezomo said.

Yeanue sputtered to a stop. "No," he said, shaking his head. "You not going nowhere. Not before I find out why you na come to our village."

6

One Leaf a Lifetime

Ezomo, Chimama, and Muja sat in the square with their backs facing the strange tree and their fronts facing the villagers. Three bowls of rice and meat sat before them. Above them, in the sky, daylight was losing its strength and yielding to night.

Ezomo eyed the children in the crowd. Some children sat with apathy. Some sat with impatience. And some, Ezomo saw, sat with contentment—perhaps happy to know they were not the ones with the sick mother, or the mother who couldn't cook, or the ones with the father who couldn't speak. For a moment, Ezomo wished to swap places. To sit with happiness in his eyes and eat his rice in peace.

"Don't eat the food," Chimama whispered. "We don't know what they put in it."

Ezomo stared at the rice and meat drizzled with palm oil. His mind strayed back to Yatta. Had she eaten today? Had anyone given her water to drink? He pushed the bowl away.

"What's wrong with the food?" asked Yeanue, pacing before them. "Eat!"

"Unh-unh. We're not hungry," Chimama said.

"I said eat!"

Chimama grabbed a small handful of rice and forced it down. Muja swallowed a piece of meat. Ezomo kept his head bowed. His mind was still with Yatta.

"Look inside my mouth!" Yeanue demanded. "How many teeth do you see?" He opened his mouth wide.

Ezomo, coming back to himself, stretched his neck to look inside Yeanue's mouth. Muja stood so he could get a good view. Chimama counted on her fingers.

"Nine," she said.

"Yus!" Yeanue slapped his chest. "Only nine. Most people have more."

Ezomo, Chimama, and Muja traded glances.

"What happened to your other teeth?" Chimama asked.

Yeanue slapped his chest again. "I na fight plenty fights to protect our tree. People na try stealing leaves plenty times. I never lose a fight, only teeth." He narrowed his eyes and wagged his finger. "If you na come steal from our tree, maybe I will only have six teeth left, but for sure, the tree will have all its leaves."

"We didn't come to steal," insisted Ezomo. "We came—"

"Good. Then tell me why you na come to our village."

It was Chimama who started to tell their tale. First she told how Oma made them sit in the back row under the mango tree, just because of their parents' circumstances. Then she told about the leopard that killed Ezomo's father.

"Why the leopard killed his father?"

"Witchcraft!"

"Leopards don't do witchcraft!" Yeanue scoffed.

Some of the villagers laughed.

"Then how did it kill Ezomo's father?" Muja said. "It has magical powers!"

"The leopard was probably hungry. When animals can't find food, they steal food from the village, and they na even attack people. Leopards don't have magical powers, just hungry bellies."

Ezomo drew his knees close and hugged his legs. The thought of a hungry leopard attacking his father was disturbing and sickening. He wished he could unhear Yeanue's words. Because in a small corner of his heart, he kept an idea that maybe his father was still alive, somewhere. No one knew Ezomo had this idea tucked away. Not even Chimama or Muja. But now, after hearing Yeanue's words, he wasn't so sure it could be true.

"But it is witchcraft!" Chimama insisted. "The very day we found the leopard, Yatta fell ill. Explain that one!"

"Who's Yatta?"

"Ezomo's mother," Muja said, pointing to Ezomo.

Yeanue looked at Ezomo. "What happened to your mother?"

Slowly, Ezomo raised his head. "I don't know." He glanced at the sky. "They say she will pass when the moon is full."

"But the moon will be full tomorrow," Yeanue said.

Ezomo was silent.

Chimama carried on. She told Yeanue about her mother. She told him how Chima couldn't cook. "Not even a grain of rice!"

The crowd erupted in whispers. Some women covered their mouths with their hands.

"How long since she can't cook?" Yeanue asked.

"It happened when I was very young," said Chimama.

The orator, who had been sitting among the villagers, dashed to the front and whispered in Yeanue's ear.

Yeanue nodded. He then turned to Chimama. "How old you are?"

"Nine. Like the teeth in your mouth."

Yeanue laughed and then his face grew serious. He exchanged a glance with the orator and turned to Muja. "And you say your father can't speak for two years now?"

"Yes."

"And you say you don't know why?"

"Yes."

"And you say one day your father woke up and his voice was gone?"

"Yes."

"And you don't know where it went?"

"No one does."

The orator whispered again in Yeanue's ear, and Yeanue whispered something back.

The panic in Ezomo had returned and made him restless. The villagers had no intention of helping them find the leopard. Besides, according to Yeanue, the leopard only killed his father because it was hungry. And yet, Yeanue's explanation did not account for Chima's inability to cook, or Toba's inability to speak, or why the leopard had appeared behind the moon. It was all very puzzling, and he hadn't the strength to piece any of it together. It was best to leave, he thought, and it was best to leave now. If they ran most of the way, and if they didn't get lost in the swamp, he could at least make it back in time to sit with Yatta before she passed. He stood up. "Please. We must go."

"Sit down," Yeanue said calmly. A dull sweetness appeared in his eyes. "There is something I must tell you."

"Please. We have to leave," Ezomo repeated. He exhaled a trembling breath. "I want to see my mother."

"No! Sit down." Yeanue stamped his foot.

Ezomo remained standing.

"We want to help you," Yeanue said, glancing at the orator. He turned to the tree and patted the trunk. "This is not a regular tree. This tree can help you. This tree can erase all your suffering."

The villagers began whispering among themselves again, and Ezomo saw that their faces had grown sullen. He looked at Yeanue, at the strange tree. The funny feeling in his stomach stirred.

"How can a tree erase our suffering?" Ezomo asked.

"I will show you!" Yeanue searched the crowd, finally resting on a boy with a sly smile. "Come here!"

The boy sprung up, scuttled to the front, and stood beside Yeanue.

"Speak for us," Yeanue said to the boy.

When the boy opened his mouth, a man's voice rushed out. The man spoke with great authority and filled the boy's eyes with pride.

Muja clutched his chest. "That . . . that's my father's voice!"

Yeanue bowed his head. "We didn't know."

Muja looked around with wide eyes. "You didn't know what?"

"That's the thing I na want to explain. This boy name is Momo. All his life, he can't speak. Just born that way. For years, Momo wished for words. Just small words. Just enough to say hello to people. When Momo turned seven, he came to the tree with a desire for a strong voice. The tree na grant it to him. But—" Yeanue inhaled deeply. "But when the tree gives here, it takes someplace else."

"What do you mean?" said Chimama. She looked at Ezomo and Muja with panic in her eyes.

"We never know from where the tree takes," Yeanue said. "That is why we only let children pick from the tree. And only one leaf a lifetime. And only if they have a true suffering. We're good people."

Some villagers nodded. Some echoed Yeanue's words. "We're good people. We're good people."

Yeanue patted Momo's back. "Go sit down."

The boy hurried past Muja and disappeared in the crowd.

Muja was stunned. He stood silent, his face pale. It was Ezomo who had to speak on his behalf. "So that boy has Toba's voice?"

Yeanue nodded. "Toba is his father? Yus, I think so. But we didn't know. We never know from where the tree takes."

Ezomo eyed the tree. This was the evil thing behind the door. He felt sick. "How come—"

"You're the thief!" Muja blurted. "You stole my father's voice!"

"We didn't know the tree na take your father's voice."

"Did you take my mother's cooking?" Chimama said, her face tight with anger.

Yeanue scanned the crowd of villagers once more and rested his eyes on a tall girl wearing a yellow lappa. "That's Amara," he said, pointing.

All eyes turned to see the girl.

"When Amara was ten, her mother discovered that Amara had no desire to cook. Amara would see a pot and run."

Someone laughed, and Yeanue paused to let the laughter depart, and once it did, he proceeded. "One day, Amara came to our tree crying. She begged the tree for skilled cooking hands. The tree na grant it to her."

Chimama's jaw dropped. "You took my mother cooking?"

"Not us. The tree took it. We are good people. We never know from where the tree takes."

Chimama covered her face with her palms and began to cry.

Ezomo struggled to speak. "Did . . . did anyone ask the tree for a father?"

Yeanue shook his head quickly. "No."

"What about a mother?"

"Never." Yeanue began pacing. "We will fix everything." A wicked grin appeared on Yeanue's face. "We will let each of you pick a leaf!"

Ezomo flinched. He looked wide-eyed at Chimama and Muja, then at Yeanue. "Huh?"

"Yus! We will." Yeanue pointed to the tree. "As you can see, we don't have many leaves left. Only thirteen. But we will let you have three. That way—" He pointed to Muja. "That way you can ask the tree to give your father back his voice." He turned to Chimama. "And you can ask the tree to give your mother back her cooking." He rested his eyes on Ezomo. "From you, we took nothing. But we are good people, so we'll let you pick a leaf anyway. That way, you can ask the tree to make your mother better."

The weight on Ezomo's back tumbled off. His mind ran out of the square, through the farm, across the swamp, and opened the village door. It ran through the forest, down the wide mud road to the gravel path, and from there to his hut where he found Yatta. She was no longer lying on the earth, gasping for air. She was boiling cassava, a smile on her worn face.

"So the tree will give my father back his voice?" asked Muja.

"Yus. Your father will speak with such power, lions will answer when he calls."

Small light appeared in Muja's eyes. "Really?"

"Yus! You will see for yourself."

Muja smiled.

"And my mother will be able to cook again?" Chimama asked.

"Yus. Her food will be the sweetest in the whole village. Kings will come from far places to taste her food."

Chimama covered her mouth and smiled.

"Who will pick first?" Yeanue asked.

These words brought Ezomo back from Sesa.

"Ezomo will go first," declared Muja.

Chimama nodded. "I'll go after Ezomo."

"And I'll go after you," Muja said.

"Good." Yeanue looked at Ezomo. "Come pick a leaf."

Ezomo inched forward. He saw that all the villagers were watching him. Some faces showed confusion. Others encouraging smiles. A few villagers beckoned him to go forth and pick a leaf.

Ezomo hesitated. "What . . . what . . . what will

happen when I pick a leaf?" he asked.

"You will need to hurry home and give it to your mother to swallow," said Yeanue.

"What will happen once she swallows it?"

"When she na swallow the leaf, she will fall asleep. By morning, the leaf will give your mother back her health."

A small smile appeared on Ezomo's lips. "She will be healthy again?"

"Yus."

The smile vanished as a horrible thought hit Ezomo. "Will the tree take from someone else?"

"Yus."

"What will it take?"

"A mother."

Ezomo felt his stomach sink. "A mother . . ."

"Yus. Someone, someplace else, will lose a mother."

Ezomo stared at Muja and then at Chimama, and then at the tree. He stepped forward one step. Ten more steps put him face-to-face with the strange tree. The trunk was really a dark blue, like the color of midnight. The bark was smooth. The leaves weren't leaves at all. They were pods—all of them green except for a yellow one with orange veins.

Ezomo touched one of the pods. It felt hairy and prickly. "Just pull it," he heard Yeanue say.

But Ezomo did not pull it for his mind had left him again, traveling once more in the direction of his village. This time, it stayed in the forest, in the grove where Yatta had fed him a bitter concoction to loosen his grief. The place where he had learned that his father was not among the strongest men who took part in the hunting contest. That he had been merely waiting to tote the load of the hunters when the leopard attacked him.

"The leopard . . ." Ezomo turned and looked at Yeanue.

"What you na say about the leopard?"

"There was a great famine the year my father died," said Ezomo. "Many crops and animals died. There was no food. The leopard must have been hungry like you said."

Yeanue's eyes widened. "I never said that!"

"You said the leopard attacked my father because it was hungry."

"You na calling me liar?"

"Did anyone ask the tree for crops?" said Ezomo.

Yeanue pursed his lips. He glanced at the tree then at the crowd.

A chicken scuttled past and clucked.

"Twice," Yeanue said.

Muja's mouth fell open. "You mean you stole our crops too?"

"Not us! The tree! The tree stole them!"

It was in this moment that a great knowing came to Ezomo. It was a knowing so disturbing that he resolved to bury it deep so that he himself would forget where he hid it and why he buried it, but that was impossible, he knew, for it was a knowing too big to hide and too stubborn to restrain—a knowing of rights relying on wrongs. Of good hinging on bad. Of tears fattening smiles.

"You did take something from me," Ezomo mumbled.

"No," Yeanue said, stamping his foot. "The tree did."

Ezomo turned to the villagers. His tears started to fall. "You're not good people."

The villagers kept quiet. Some bowed their heads.

"Muja was right." Ezomo turned to Yeanue. "You *are* thieves. All of you."

"Fine! My first duty as a thief is to steal a new wrapper for you!" Yeanue laughed.

A few villagers laughed with him. But many remained

silent, their faces besieged with sorrow.

Yeanue carried on laughing, slapping his thigh and jumping around, his snorts thickening and stretching and halting only after he guided his eyes to the small group of villagers in the back of the crowd and saw them staring at him gravely.

"Um-hum," he said, clearing the remaining glee in his throat. "We will fix the thing we spoiled. You only need to pick a leaf."

Ezomo felt a great emptiness from all he had lost, and all he was going to lose. But he also felt full, for he knew more now than before, and though what he knew disturbed him, it also brought him peace. He understood that his past would never become his present. His father would never rise from the soil. He had to accept the *now*, as ugly as it was, for it was all he had. He would drop the load of yesterday, and carry only the one of today, which was plenty enough to hold. And more importantly, he would treasure the small belief he still had left. Believing had turned Dragonfly into a stone. It was possible, maybe, that his belief had power too.

"Pick a leaf," Yeanue demanded.

"No," said Ezomo.

"No?" Yeanue scratched his head. "You want your mother to die?"

Ezomo closed his eyes. *Who stole your wings small bird? Who stole your pride? Get up and try, get up and fly. Dry the shame from your eyes small bird. Get up and try, get up and fly.*

"What are you mumbling?" Yeanue said, looking around puzzled. "Don't you want her to live?"

Ezomo opened his eyes. "Yes. I do," he said. "More than anything. But I can't take someone else's mother so that I can keep mine." He looked Yeanue in the eye. "I'm not like you."

Ezomo turned and walked away from Yeanue, away from the tree, away from the villagers. And out of the village square.

"What . . . what . . . what about you?" Yeanue mumbled to Muja. "Don't you want to give your father back his voice?" He looked at Chimama. "And . . . and . . . and don't you want your mother to cook?"

"We're not thieves like you," Muja said. "Come Chimama." He took her hand. Together, they followed Ezomo.

7
Going Home

By the time Ezomo, Chimama, and Muja reached the creek separating the village from the farm, they were out of breath, having raced most of the way. Fireflies flashed their lights. Grasshoppers scratched their wings. The air, warm and breezy, smelled of day and night—of one thing ending and another beginning.

"We must hurry!" Ezomo said. "We must reach the door before night arrives."

They dashed through the fruit trees and across the sweet potato field, their hearts fearing the consequences of returning home empty-handed. They were farmers returning from the field without crops. Fishermen returning from the river without fish. Hunters returning from the forest without meat.

The sweet potato field gave way to the cassava field, and the cassava field gave way to the sugarcane farm, and at the end of the farm, the friends met the swamp.

"Wait!"

They turned and saw Yeanue running toward them. Following him was the orator holding a torch and behind him was a long line of villagers.

"Wait!"

In Yeanue's right hand was a thing he waved in the air. A thing they could not see, so they waited for Yeanue to come closer, and when he did, they saw he was holding a leaf.

"You na earn it," he said, offering the leaf to Ezomo, Chimama, and Muja.

Muja crossed his arms. "We want nothing from your tree."

"It's not like the other leaves," explained Yeanue, panting. "This one is different. It's the golden leaf. Grows only every six years. It gives, but never takes."

"It gives, but never takes?" Ezomo said with wide eyes.

"Yus. Here, take it."

Ezomo took the leaf from Yeanue and rubbed his thumb against it. The leaf felt smooth, not prickly, and inside it, he felt the gathering of many tiny seeds.

Muja stepped forward. "So this leaf will not steal from someplace else? And my father's voice will return when he swallows it?"

"Yus."

"And my mother will cook again?" Chimama asked.

"Yus!"

Ezomo's eyes grew big and bright. "And my mother will live?"

"Yus!"

"But how will all three of them swallow it?" Muja asked.

Yeanue shook his head. "All three cannot swallow it. Only one."

"Then we need three golden leaves. One for Yatta, one for Chima, and one for my father," Muja said angrily.

"Let Ezomo have it since his mother is dying," Yeanue suggested.

Chimama turned to Ezomo. Her eyes were wet. "You and Yatta need the leaf. But me and my mother need it too."

The villagers began to grumble. Some said it was best for Chimama to have the leaf for it was a great shame that her mother couldn't even boil rice. "Chimama deserves the leaf!" they chanted.

"No! My father deserves the leaf," Muja sputtered. "I want Yatta to live, and I want Chima to cook, but I also want my father to speak. We're suffering too."

The villagers grumbled again. Some reasoned it was best for Muja to have the leaf for it was a great shame for a man to have no voice. "Give it to Muja!" they yelled.

Ezomo turned pale. His mother deserved the leaf, but so did Chima and Toba.

Yeanue jumped up. "I have the answer! Give your mother the leaf, and once she's well, she can cook for Chimama's mother and speak for Muja's father."

Chimama turned to Ezomo. "What kind of food can Yatta cook?"

"Um . . . um . . . she makes good cassava bread," he said.

Chimama twisted her mouth. "I don't like cathava bread."

"And Yatta can't speak for my father," Muja said. "A man needs a man's voice."

Chimama narrowed her eyes. "If you don't give me that leaf, I will no longer be your friend."

"And if you don't give *me* the leaf," Muja said, "I will never speak to you again."

Ezomo closed his eyes. He saw himself eating a mango with Chimama and Muja. He saw the three of them chasing the leopard in the forest. He saw them sliding down the kapok trunk. He saw them sitting together under Oma's mango tree. He saw Chimama holding him while he wept. He saw Muja patting his back. He saw the three of them hugging on the sugarcane farm. Ezomo dropped the golden leaf.

Yeanue dove for it, grabbing it out of the mud. "Have you lost your mind? Don't you want the leaf?"

Ezomo opened his eyes. "No."

The crowd of villagers gasped.

"You take it then," Yeanue said, giving the leaf to Chimama.

Chimama snatched the leaf. She squeezed it. She smiled, then frowned. She turned to Muja. "You have it."

Muja took it. He glanced at the leaf lying in the shadow of his palm. He whispered something in Chimama's ear. She whispered something back.

"Muja and I have a mother and a father," Chimama said to Ezomo. "If Yatta dies, you'll have neither."

"Here!" Muja said, holding out the golden leaf. "Give it to Yatta!"

Ezomo looked at Chimama and Muja. His face glowed with shock.

"Maybe there's still time to save Yatta," Chimama said.

Ezomo lifted the leaf carefully from Muja's palm.

"Thank you," he said, embracing Muja, then Chimama.

Yeanue grinned, showing all nine of his teeth. "I will keep a golden leaf for each of you," he said to Chimama and Muja. "Don't worry. Come back in six years. And then six years after that. You will see."

"We will see," Muja said.

Chimama nodded. "Uh-huh, we will."

Ezomo turned and ran then, trampling cattails and splashing mud as he jumped into the swamp. Frogs and fish scattered as he darted by. A crake bird resting in a shrub squealed and took off. The breeze raced behind Ezomo. And so did Chimama and Muja. They hurried into the cool night and disappeared behind a bend.

"Are we good people now?" they heard Yeanue shout.

Ezomo, Chimama, and Muja ran through the sour water, going this way and that way, turning here and turning there, doing their best to remember the way home. News spread across the swamp that the children were back and that they were no longer chasing after the leopard. They now had a leaf, which according to them, could mend any suffering. The lizards, after hearing the news, said the children had gained some wisdom, for a leopard could not hide behind the moon, but a plant could cure a suffering. For once, the crake birds agreed with the lizards. They said that the children were indeed wiser for when they, the crake birds, whispered in their ears to go here and go there, turn this way but not that way, the children listened well and followed their instructions, so that it was possible to guide them safely back to the village door.

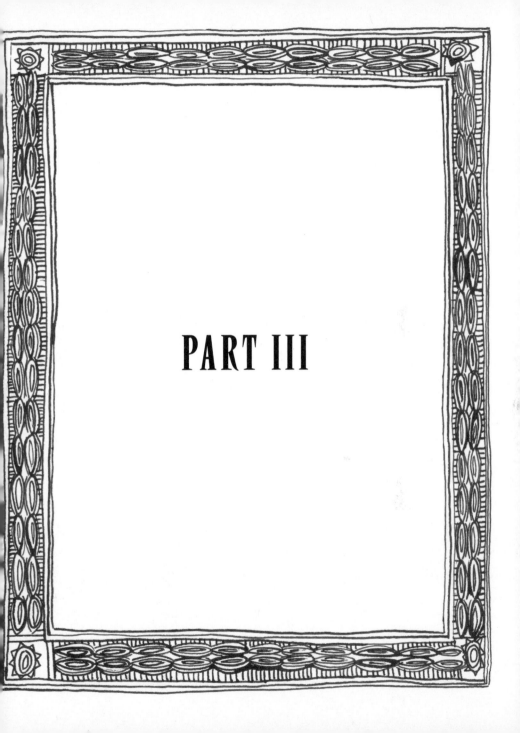

PART III

I

The Whole Story

For two whole days, the village of Sesa had turned upside down. There was no cooking or quarreling under the Palaver Hut, no meetings by the riverbank, and no lessons under the mango tree. Everyone hid in their huts, terrified of the evil thing about to seep through the village door. Chickens held their clucks. Goats held their bleats. The breeze held its blow. Even the kingfisher birds stayed in their burrows, abandoning their habit of carrying news far. All except Bisa—he was perched in a tree at the edge of the forest.

Near where Bisa perched, the Elders, hunters, and a handful of villagers gathered around a fire to wait for the children to return, their faces tired and weary, their heads itching with questions only Ezomo, Muja, and Chimama could scratch. In their midst were Chima and Toba, both burdened with a heavy sadness nobody could lift.

As they waited, the people of Sesa discussed what to do once the children arrived. Some suggested sending them straight to the Valley. Others wanted to hear what they had seen behind the door before sending them away. Chima begged the Elders to forgive the children and send them home. Toba knelt before them with clasped hands and pleaded silently.

Finally, the Elders announced a plan. The children, should they return, would be ordered to share what they'd seen. They would then be sent to the Valley. As far as forgiveness, the Elders spoke with clear throats when they told Toba and Chima that even if the sun and the moon came down from the sky to plead for the children, they would still send Ezomo, Chimama, and Muja to the Valley. Absolutely nothing would change their minds.

Ezomo, Chimama, and Muja huddled behind the village door, deliberating what to do. Around them, the night darkened. The air cooled. Now and then, a firefly shared its light, then melted away.

Ezomo thought they should sneak to his hut and give Yatta the leaf. Muja thought it best to show the leaf to the Elders before giving it to Yatta. It was possible, Muja reasoned, that the Elders would forgive them after hearing about the strange tree and the villagers who stole their crops. He suggested they go straight to the Elders and tell them the whole story.

Chimama had another idea. She wanted to open the door, run to Noroad, and grab Chima and Toba. Together they would then visit Yatta, and if Yatta was all right, they would take the leaf to the Elders and tell them about the tree. If Yatta appeared to be near death, they would give her the leaf, but at least Toba and Chima—having seen the leaf themselves—could vouch that they were telling the truth.

Ezomo, Chimama, and Muja deliberated, taking a piece of one idea and mashing it with another, keeping this and tossing that, sifting out the bad and straining the good, until finally, they had a plan they believed in.

2

A Disturbing Sound

It was Ezomo who opened the door, peeking through first with the right eye before permitting the left eye to join. Together, both eyes saw a dim forest with dead trees lying on the soil. Moonlight gathered on some bushes. Darkness gathered on the others. The air smelled wet.

"Nobody's here," Ezomo whispered, squeezing through. Chimama and Muja followed. They stepped over the scattered trunks, their bodies trembling with fear. The forest was the boar, they the impalas.

Moonlight guided them through thick mimosa bushes, up low hills, and along grassy footpaths. They ran and ran, carrying on their backs the hope of saving Yatta and the hope of being called heroes, for though they had no leopard, they knew why Chima couldn't cook and why Toba couldn't speak. And they knew why the crops were dying.

There was no telling what time of the night it was when their plan began to spoil. Not long after passing a dry creek bed and then a giant ant mound, they heard a disturbing sound. They heard clapping.

Six feet stopped. Three noses held their breath. Standing there stunned, they heard the clapping again, like sticks slamming trees. Ezomo saw a figure in the bush, holding a machete.

"Oh!" Ezomo exclaimed and ducked. Chimama and Muja ducked with him.

The figure stepped forward, and then stepped back. It raised the machete.

"Papa?" Muja said, starting to stand. "Papa!" He sprang up and ran forward.

The figure pressed a finger against its lips, then rushed to hug Muja.

Slowly, Ezomo stood. "It's Toba," he whispered. Chimama stood too.

After hugging all three children, Toba frowned and tapped his head.

Muja nodded solemnly. "He says we've done a very stupid thing."

Looking around nervously, Toba shook his head while pointing to the edge of the forest.

"He says we can't go that way," Muja translated for his father. "The Elders and Hunters are waiting for us there."

"Is my mother okay?" Ezomo asked.

Toba shook his head and raised his shoulders.

Chimama bit her bottom lip, then asked, "Are the Elders angry?"

"He says they're planning to send us to the Valley."

Toba shook his machete in the air.

"He says they'll have to kill him first before he lets them take any of us."

Ezomo felt his stomach tie itself into knots. Toba was speaking of death. Were both Toba and Yatta going to die before the night was over? He flung the thought out of his head.

"Tell him the plan!" Ezomo urged Muja. But Muja didn't hear Ezomo. He was busy telling his father about the strange tree.

". . . then the tree gave it to the boy," Muja was saying.

"In six years, we can go get a leaf for you. Then you will speak again!"

"Tell him the plan!" Ezomo repeated.

And Muja tried. But after motioning the children to follow, Toba hurried ahead with a plan of his own.

3

News to Carry

The land climbed high, flattened, then tilted down, taking with it Ezomo, Muja, Chimama, and Toba. They scrambled down the hill, reached the bottom, and crossed a pit left by the roots of a fallen tree. They hurried forward, passing a young impala sleeping near a stream and then a deserted hut overgrown with climbing weeds.

"Chimama?"

That's what they heard not too long after passing the hut. They stopped, going no farther than they already were.

"Chimama!"

Standing with the night was Chima, a cooking spoon in her hand.

"Mamie!" Chimama ran to her mother.

"*Shhh* . . . ," someone there that night whispered.

Mother and daughter embraced, then cried, then embraced some more. "Are you all right?" Chima asked.

Chimama nodded. "I know what happened to—"

"You've done a terrible thing," Chima said. "A very terrible thing!"

Chimama bowed her head.

"De Elders want to send you to de Valley." Chima wagged the spoon in the air. "But de Elders will have to get through me first!"

"Have you seen my mother?" Ezomo asked.

Chima shook her head. "We will hide them on de farm," she told Toba.

Toba nodded and held up one finger. Then he pointed far in the distance.

"One night on the farm," Muja translated. "Tomorrow, we'll hide them near the Valley."

"Good idea," Chima said. "No one will think to look for them there."

"What about my mother?" Ezomo said, opening his palm to reveal the golden leaf. "I need to give this to her. It will make her well." In the dark, the leaf looked like a leaf from any other tree. It showed no signs of possessing magic, and Ezomo wondered if it even did.

Toba shook his head and pounded his fist.

"He says there's no time. He says we must hide now."

"No!" Ezomo shook Muja's shoulder. "I need to see my mother."

Toba crossed his heart and pointed to the leaf. And just as Muja turned to tell Ezomo what his father said, something terrible happened.

Earlier that night, Toba had left the group of villagers waiting near the edge of the forest. He'd backed away to try to reach the children before the children reached the villagers. He managed to leave without anyone seeing him—anyone except for Chima, who had followed Toba when she saw him sneaking away. What Chima didn't know was that someone else was watching, too.

Bisa had spotted Toba passing by, and moments later, Chima. He thought it no coincidence that the parents of the missing children were creeping away together. So Bisa followed behind Chima, and when he heard her shout "Chimama!" and when he saw the three children, his eyes glinted. His ears tingled. He snapped his beak closed and flew out of the forest. This was news he intended to carry.

4

A Big Commotion

Ezomo, Chimama, and Muja followed Chima and Toba through the elephant grass, walked around the outskirts of the main compound, crossed the gravel path, then reached the farm. Cassava and yams huddled on their plot. Mango trees leaned against the night. On the other side of the grassy field, moonlight rested on the river.

The air reeked of smoke, and Ezomo thought he heard a whisper. He paused and stepped back. He stretched his eyes wide and spotted a shadow. He took another step back, bumping into Chima and Chimama. Toba still crept ahead, Muja following him.

"I think somebody's—"

Before Ezomo could finish, a swarm of hunters rose from the field.

Ezomo turned and ran, passing Chimama and Chima, who stood gawking at the sight. "Run!" Ezomo shouted.

Muja, who had stopped when he heard Ezomo's warning, saw Toba struggling with three hunters. He raced to help his father but was grabbed by another hunter who pinned him to the soil. "Let me go!" Muja screamed and bit the hunter's arm, managing to flee briefly before two more hunters wrestled him to the ground.

Chima ran to help Chimama who was being carried away. She knocked the spoon on the hunter's head so hard that he dropped Chimama and cowered. She helped Chimama up, and they ran back in the direction of the trees. Two hunters ran after them. More followed. And soon they'd caught the mother and daughter like they'd caught the father and son.

Ezomo ran with all his might. He ran for himself. He ran for Yatta. He ran to bury his past. And he ran to see his future. He ran to escape doubt. He ran to meet hope. He ran with all his strength and all his weaknesses too. He ran for today, and he ran for tomorrow. He ran to forget his shame. He ran to reclaim his pride. But the hunters knew none of these things, and so one of them grabbed Ezomo. And another came to help. And together, they captured him for good.

5
Next Came the Trial

The hunters plunked Ezomo, Muja, and Chimama under the same mango tree where Oma gave her lessons. Surrounding them were the Elders, hunters, a handful of villagers holding torches, and Sao the orator. Toba and Chima sat nearby with nine hunters guarding them. Someone lit a fire. Someone passed around water.

"Tell us what you saw behind the door!" Sao demanded.

Ezomo stared at the faces in front of him. He saw eyes filled with anger and eyes filled with pity. He also saw eyes filled with envy and wondered why *anyone* would be envious of him. He drew his legs in and hugged his knees. The air was warm and smoky and heavy with the smell of ripe mangos. Suddenly, he was overcome with a strange desire to see Oma—to sit against the mango tree and listen to her speak. But Oma wasn't there, and neither were any of her pupils. They were in their huts sleeping like good children. Was he the bad one?

"Where is my mother?" Ezomo asked.

"I'll ask the questions, not you!" snapped Sao.

Ezomo sprung up. "Is she still alive?" he managed to say before a hunter shoved him down.

Sao turned to the villagers behind him. "Where is Yatta?"

Most of them shrugged. One man said he'd seen Yatta that morning in the market. Another said he saw Yatta by the river. A third said both men were mistaken for Yatta was unwell and in her hut—she was expected to die if she hadn't already.

"Are you sending us to the Valley?" Chimama asked.

Sao laughed. "Are we sending you to the Valley? Does the moon shine at night?"

Chimama buried her head in her lap.

"Don't cry," Muja said, putting his arm around Chimama, though he too began to weep.

Sao wagged his finger at Ezomo. "If you want to see your mother, tell us what you found behind the village door."

☒ ☒ ☒

So Ezomo told the whole story from beginning to end, starting with the day he saw the leopard in the forest. He told them of the night they went to the Valley to see Ada. He told them how they opened the village door to follow the leopard and discovered a swamp.

"A swamp?" asked Sao with big, curious eyes.

"Yes," said Ezomo.

"What kind of a swamp?" Sao continued. "Did it hold spirits?"

"No."

Wrinkles stretched across Sao's forehead. "What then did you see?"

"Only mosquitos, frogs, lizards, and birds. And the leopard."

"What leopard?"

Ezomo pointed to the sky. "A leopard hiding behind the moon."

"You making fun of us?" said Sao, fuming. "You have one last chance to tell us the truth!"

Muja spoke then and said that Ezomo *was* telling the truth. They had all seen a leopard behind the moon, or a moon turned into a leopard, one of the two.

Sao wiped his palm over his face. "What did you really see huh? Tell us!"

What Ezomo said next caused a great stir. He told them about the village of Ekewe, about its bald citizens and its strange tree. But the greatest excitement came when he told them about the boy who possessed Toba's voice, and the girl who possessed Chima's cooking.

"He's lying!" one of the Elders shouted. The villagers pressed in, crowding Ezomo, Chimama, and Muja, pointing and shouting. Someone waved a torch in Ezomo's face. Someone flung dirt at Muja. A grandmother named Mah threw herself on the ground, pulling her hair and screaming. "Send these wicked children away!"

Villagers who had been asleep came running to see what was stirring under the mango tree. Oma came too. "You've shamed me!" she said, jabbing her chewing stick in Ezomo's face. "Didn't you learn anything under my tree?"

"They have threatened our existence!" Muna hollered.

Bisa zipped to and fro. "They found them! Come and see!" he screeched. "They're here!"

◪ ◪ ◪

"Quiet, everyone!" It took Sao some time to bring order back to the mango tree. "So you're telling me these villagers stole Toba's voice and Chima's cooking?" Sao asked once the villagers settled.

"Yes," said Ezomo quietly. "And more too."

"Don't believe anything he says!" Oma bellowed.

"*Shhh . . .*" Sao leaned close to Ezomo. "What more is there?" he whispered.

Ezomo pointed to the field. "They stole our crops!"

"Ha-ya!" Sao jumped back. "Are you mocking us again?"

"Show them the leaf!" Muja said.

Ezomo unclenched his fist, revealing a tiny leaf.

Sao froze then leaned forward cautiously. "What is that?"

"The golden leaf!" Ezomo held the leaf high. "From their tree."

"Move back, everyone! Move back!" Sao ordered, his arms spread to make a barrier between the villagers and Ezomo. "Quick! Move!"

The villagers scuttled back. Some of them hid behind tree trunks. The hunters drew their machetes.

"It can erase any suffering!" Ezomo shouted.

"Silence!" Spit spewed from Sao's mouth. "You wicked,

wicked boy! How dare you bring this great evil to Sesa. You are more than useless!"

Ezomo lowered his arm. "I'm not useless!"

"Maybe the boy is telling the truth!" It was Old Man Flomo. He pointed to the largest plot on the farm—the one filled with dust and weeds. "Our crops *are* dying!"

"Give me that leaf!" Sao ordered without any attention to Flomo's remarks.

Two hunters inched closer to Ezomo, their machetes flashing.

"No!" said Ezomo, looking around at the villagers. "This leaf will save my mother." Flame flickered on the faces watching him. They were angry faces. And sad faces. And faces overwhelmed with fear. He felt frightened too. But he also felt brave. He had seen things none of them had. He had shown courage where most of them would have cowered. Ezomo stood tall. "Let me see my mother!"

But the leaf was pried out of Ezomo's palm, then given to Sao, who marveled at it with open mouth before tucking it in the waist of his wrapper.

"Give it back!" Ezomo cried.

"Take him to the Valley now!" Sao ordered. "All three of them!"

Chima wailed. She pleaded with the Elders to forgive the children. Toba held Sao's feet and begged, and still, they wouldn't relent.

"We're telling the truth!" Muja screamed as two hunters dragged him away.

"Leave me alone!" Chimama yelled.

"Please don't punish Chimama and Muja. It's all my fault," Ezomo pleaded. "They were only trying to help me."

Ezomo, Chimama, and Muja were scooped up and carried over the shoulders of hunters, away from the farm and to the river, then to the forsaken stretch of road leading to the Valley. Some villagers followed for a while, their shouts and jeers weakening, their voices changing from plenty to few, becoming smaller and smaller until they disappeared.

6

Return to the Valley

Finally the hunters, who had grown tired of carrying the children, ordered them to walk. And so they walked and walked and walked. They walked until the dirt path turned them over to the rocky road, and the rocky road turned them over to the gritty field, and the field stretched wide and far, then delivered them to the Valley.

"Please let us go!" Ezomo pleaded when they arrived.

But the hunters did not let them go. Instead, they shoved Ezomo, Chimama, and Muja into the kapok tree and sent them sliding down to that forsaken place.

The shadows of coconut trees played in small light borrowed from the moon. Cold air roamed freely and shook the witchweeds resting in the dry streambed.

Ezomo staggered toward an anthill with light flickering inside. Chimama and Muja trundled behind him. "They're gone!" he heard someone say. It was then that he saw heads poking out of the giant anthills. An old woman limped into the moonlight. A man carrying a bucket wandered out and stood by the dry stream. One woman asked if they were lost. Another asked if they were hungry.

"Welcome home!" It was Ada, pushing her way through, Ofasa and Humongous beside her. She wobbled forward and stood near the three children, her bright eyes jumping from face to face. She cupped her mouth, then uncupped it. "Where did the three of you go?"

"You left us!" Chimama blurted.

"You lied!" Muja added.

Ada grabbed Ofasa's hand and nudged him behind her. "Did you catch the leopard?" she said, giggling. "Let's play a game!" She turned to Ofasa. "Go get the ball."

"We don't want to play!" Chimama snapped.

Ada's smile vanished. "You don't?"

"You got us in big trouble!" said Chimama.

"You said you would help us!" Muja sputtered. "You lied!"

Ofasa came running back with the ball. It wasn't a true ball, though, just clumps of dead grass tied with bamboo. Ada took it and smiled, then gave it back to Ofasa. "They don't want to play." The glow in Ofasa's eyes retreated.

"I thought you were our friend!" Chimama said.

Ada snatched Chimama's arm. "I am your friend!" she said, squeezing.

Chimama yanked her arm from Ada's grip. "You're not!"

"Selfish children! You only think of yourself. What about me, huh?" The veins on Ada's forehead puckered. "Don't I miss my mother and father too?"

"Why did you leave us in the swamp?" asked Ezomo, stepping forward.

"Why did you leave us in the swamp?" Ada mocked. "So you can suffer like me! You think it's fair for you to go home to your mothers and fathers while I suffer here alone?"

"Old Woman!" Humongous screeched.

Muja's mouth fell open. "You intended to get us in trouble?"

Ada grinned.

Ezomo shook his head gravely. "That's why you wanted us to open the door."

"Yes. That's why I hid behind the cattails in the swamp. I was sure you spotted me, but you didn't. Thought you would get scared and return to Sesa when you noticed I was gone. Then the Elders would punish you. But you didn't follow the plan, did you?" She shrugged. "Doesn't matter. In the end, I got what I wanted, didn't I?"

Chimama turned pale. "You're more wicked than the people of Ekewe."

"You betrayed these little children." Humongous flapped away from Ada and perched on a coconut tree. "You lied to me too."

"Me, me, me. Selfish! All of you. What about Ada huh?" Ada's eyes glowed with bitter tears. "Do I deserve to suffer like this?"

"No!" Humongous said sternly. "But you can't cast your hurt on other people. Your heart will never heal that way. It will only grow darker."

Ada dried her eyes. "Too late."

"Maybe not. Maybe the children will forgive you,"

Humongous said, swooping down and landing near Ada's feet.

Muja looked away. Chimama crossed her arms.

Ezomo looked at Ada. Tears rolled down her face. Her frail body sagged. The bandage around her leg had unraveled, and the tail of the cloth dragged in the dirt. He felt angry. But he also felt sorry. Ada really did do an awful thing. But it was because of Ada that he found the tree. It was because of Ada that he earned the golden leaf.

"We found something strange," Ezomo said. "A tree."

Ada dried her eyes. "What tree?" She wiped her nose.

"Behind the door. In a village. We found the tree that took Chimama's mother's cooking and Muja's father's voice. It's the reason our crops are dying."

Mischief flashed in Ada's eyes. "A witch tree! Where behind the door?"

"You did a very bad thing, Ada." Ezomo sighed. "But because of you, we found the tree."

Ada smirked. "You mean wicked Ada helped you?"

Ezomo hesitated. "I wouldn't—"

"So you'll be my friend?"

Chimama crossed her arms. "You betrayed us! We're not your friends."

"Say you're sorry, Old Woman!" Humongous ordered.

"I'm sorry," Ada blurted.

"Say it like you mean it!" Humongous snapped.

"I'm very, very sorry." Ada pressed her palm on her heart. "I really am."

"You better be!" Chimama said, letting her arms fall to her sides.

"Can you help us out of here?" Ezomo asked, scanning the area and looking for the narrow passageway.

Ada stepped forward with confidence. "Where do you want to go?"

"To find Sao."

He needed to seize the golden leaf from Sao, Ezomo explained. Then he needed to take it to his mother. He glanced at the sky. The morning was approaching, and the moon would soon set. It was nearly stuffed, Ezomo saw, and when it reappeared in the evening, it would be all the way full. There was still time to save his mother if nobody interfered.

"We'll send Humongous," Ada suggested. "He's small.

No one will see him." She turned to the bird. "Find Sao and get that leaf! Then bring it here."

"Hurry! Please!" Ezomo begged after telling Humongous where Sao lived.

And Humongous, having all the information he needed, soared out of the Valley.

7
A Very Big Job

Humongous had never performed a task as big as the one asked of him that day. His heart throbbed as he soared out of the Valley. He would finally prove that his big name was no mistake.

Humongous soared above the rocky path, passing bald hills and bare trees, piercing streaks of daylight. He whizzed past the river, past a fisherman unmooring his canoe. Soon he reached the farm and heard a hoe loosening soil. He flew on, among the creaking and crinkling of a morning settling, stopping only when he reached the compound of the Elders.

Sao lived in the third hut, the one with a pepper garden. Sao usually slept under a palm tree in his yard, Ezomo had said, but on this day, Humongous found no one under the tree or anywhere in the compound. The compound was still.

Humongous flew behind Sao's hut, perched on the roof, and listened. Under the thatch, he heard the careless snore of a contented sleeper. He fluttered to the ledge of the window and spied Sao asleep on his mat. It was in that moment that Humongous's big courage grew small. How could a tiny kingfisher bird like him seize anything from a big man like Sao? It was wise to wait. Eventually, Sao would rise for his morning bath, and Humongous would follow him and snatch the leaf. He folded his wings and waited.

Before the sun came up, Humongous heard shuffling coming from Sao's hut. He watched the orator rise from his mat, take a sip of water, and slip out of his house. Humongous flew to the top of the palm tree and from there saw Sao creeping around to the back of his hut, his feet quickening, his eyes looking over his shoulder. He then headed in the direction of the forest.

When Sao arrived at the edge of the forest, Humongous saw him stop before a bush willow tree. He stretched up and plucked a small yellow leaf from the tree. Then he reached into the waist of his wrapper and retrieved the golden leaf. They looked identical, the two leaves, except one glowed, and the other didn't. Sao tucked the bush willow leaf into his wrapper. Then he buried the golden leaf under the bush willow tree and marked the spot with a stick. Humongous wasted no time. As soon as Sao had disappeared into the forest, he sped to the ground and with his sharp beak dug the leaf from the soil.

"Put that back!"

Startled, Humongous jumped.

Behind him stood Bisa.

"Awful bird!" Bisa spat, fluttering his wings. "E the one who helped Ada!"

"Who you calling awful?" Humongous sassed, letting the leaf slip from his beak.

Bisa pressed his toe on the leaf. "What e doing with the evil leaf?"

"I'm returning it to Ezomo!"

"Ha! Not with Bisa here. Nothing passes my eyes or ears!"

"Get out of my way," Humongous yelled, sweeping dirt in Bisa's face. "I have a big job to do." He snatched the leaf and took off.

"Traitor!" Bisa rose into the air.

Trrrrr . . . Humongous zipped under the branch of a quiver tree.

Bisa whizzed behind him. "Traitor!" he squawked. "Come everyone! Come quick!"

But the villagers did not come quick. They were all attending to different affairs. The men sat by the riverbank, admiring the golden leaf Sao had brought to them and discussing what to do with it. The women sat under the Palaver Hut, quarreling about Ezomo. And the children sat under the mango tree, discussing the events that had transpired the night before.

Bisa chased Humongous around the forest and cornered him in a banana tree. "Give it here, awful bird with your big-for-nothing name!" Bisa snatched the golden leaf and swooped up.

Humongous whizzed after Bisa. *Trrrrr* . . . "Bitter bird! Give it back!"

Catching up to him, Humongous pecked Bisa's head and seized the leaf. "Aha!" *Trrrrr* . . . He bolted toward the Valley with Bisa after him.

"Come back here!" Bisa yelled.

They zipped this way and that way, snatching the leaf from each other. An old man named Mobasi stood in the forest that day with his hand above his brow, grinning and giggling as he watched Bisa and Humongous fuss in the sky.

Meanwhile, Ezomo waited in the Valley. He waited with worry lining his forehead. What more could he do? He had done everything he knew to save his mother, and nothing had worked. He had tossed his net in an empty river. He had planted all his seeds on arid land. He folded his hands in his lap. He didn't know what else to do except wait and watch the sky, and hope that Humongous would return before the full moon appeared.

Humongous eventually did return. But long after he was supposed to and long after the afternoon had arrived. He was out of breath and dirty, and above his eye throbbed a fresh cut, but he had lived up to his name. He had chased Bisa into the depths of the forest, he told the children. And Bisa had chased him back.

"And what?" Ada asked impatiently.

And by narrow luck, he had managed to steal the leaf from Bisa and escape. But Bisa had alerted the hunters, and they were on their way to the Valley to take back the leaf.

"Better take it to your mother now!" Humongous warned, giving Ezomo the leaf.

So once more, Ada led the children through the narrow gully to the river and ushered Ezomo into the canoe. Humongous would guide him to the forest and then to Sesa. The rest of them would stay behind and stall the hunters.

8

The Full Moon

Sometimes the moon rises early. Sometimes it rises late. On this day, as Ezomo followed Humongous through the forest, he stopped and gaped at the sky, for on this day, of all days, the moon had arrived early. It came from nowhere. It came without care. It was big and bright and all the way full, and it rose high and covered the afternoon sky. Ezomo watched it rise. Then he sat down and closed his eyes. He saw his mother lying on the dirt floor in their hut, a smile on her face, her eyes shut. "Goodbye, Mamie," he whispered.

"Aha!" It was Bisa. "Found him!"

Ezomo's eyes remained shut, his sobs gushing through the forest.

Bisa closed his beak. "What is it, Ezomo?" he asked.

"The moon is full you stupid bird," Humongous said, pointing to the sky.

"A-hey!" Bisa said. "It's that awful bird again!"

"They said his mother would die when the moon becomes full," said Humongous.

Bisa sighed. He looked at the moon. Then at the boy sobbing. Then again at the moon.

"Ezomo! Did they say Yatta will die the instant the moon becomes full?" Bisa asked, hopping from one foot to the other. "Don't e know the moon stays full longer than a day?"

Ezomo looked up. His eyes widened.

"Give me that leaf!" Bisa said, flapping his wing. "I can get to Yatta much faster than e can."

Ezomo looked at the moon. He smiled. Bisa was right. The moon would stay full for some time. He could still save his mother. "How do I know you'll take it to her?" Ezomo asked. "You might give it to the Elders. You're cantankerous!"

Bisa clicked his beak. "I am cantankerous." He glared at Humongous. "But I'm not wicked like some other birds I know."

Humongous rolled his eyes. "Oh, please! You're just a fly sniffing for fruit!"

"E can trust me, Ezomo!" said Bisa. "Quickly!"

Ezomo looked around. Indeed, the hunters were everywhere, their voices growing and shrinking and growing and shrinking. He looked at Bisa and cringed. The bird could not be trusted, but what else was he to do? Ezomo took a deep breath and summoned his small belief. And that is how it came to be that on that day, in that forest, Ezomo turned to the most cantankerous bird he knew and gave Bisa the golden leaf. His heart drummed as he watched the bird soar toward the sky. Then, neither of them completely trusting Bisa, Ezomo and Humongous dashed after him.

9

Yatta

Not too long after Bisa flew off with the leaf, a hunter spotted Ezomo. "I found him!" the hunter shouted.

Ezomo ran, ducking behind bushes and hiding behind trees, wild footsteps following him. "Don't let him escape!" Ezomo heard the hunter yell. He lay still in the underbrush and waited for the footsteps to pass. Then he sprinted past the grove of banana trees, and jumped over a small creek, his heart filled with maybes. Maybe he would escape the hunters. Maybe Bisa would take the leaf to his mother. Maybe the bird would reach her in time. Maybe she was still alive. Maybe the Elders would forgive him. Maybe he could make his mother smile and Oma proud. And maybe everyone would see him as useful instead of useless.

When he finally reached his compound, he ducked under a clothesline of drying lappas. He heard a shy laugh and the shuffling of feet. The air was gray and smoky. Someone was frying fish. His feet scraped the red earth as he walked across the yard, passing seven huts before reaching the crooked one in the back. He searched for courage and found none, so he entered the hut with fear.

Inside, the light was dim. His eyes, anxious to rest, jumped to all the wrong places, looking first at the empty oil lamp, then at the rusty wheelbarrow, and then at two rattan baskets lying in a corner. Ezomo realized his eyes were stalling—avoiding the thing they already saw. Yatta on the earth, a blanket covering her body. His heart skipped.

Holding his breath, he rested his eyes on her face, on the lines in her skin. Her head was wrapped in a black cloth, and Ezomo saw that she was wearing a black gown. Beside her was an empty water jug. Next to it, a bowl of rice entertaining a few flies. The air smelled sour, like spoiled fruit waiting to rot.

"Mamie?" Ezomo whispered.

He heard flies buzzing over the rice. Somewhere, someone was humming a song.

Ezomo, still holding his breath, knelt beside his mother. He freed the tears he was keeping. "Mamie?"

Ezomo closed his eyes and summoned all memories of his mother. He saw her boiling cassava. He saw her giving him a mango. He saw her holding his hand in the market. He saw her washing clothes. He saw her feeding him a bitter root. He saw her smile. He saw her cry. He saw her showing him her scabbed knuckles. Ezomo lost himself in the memories, opening one door after the other, going too far to pull himself back.

"Ezomo?"

Ezomo opened his eyes.

"Ezomo?"

His mother was speaking. He looked down. He saw his mother, still lying under the blanket. Her hands neatly by her side, her head raised slightly off the ground. Her eyes open.

He rushed to hug her.

"Where have you been, Ezomo?"

Ezomo kissed her forehead. Then he hugged her three more times. He looked around the room, his eyes wide. "They said you would die . . ."

"Who said?"

"The Elders."

Yatta nodded. "I'm very, very sick."

"I brought a leaf to heal you." He lowered his head. "And then Sao took it."

Yatta drew in a long breath and coughed, then lifted her head again. "Yes, I know. Bisa told me. He brought me a leaf to swallow. Said you went behind the door to get it. Said if I swallowed it, I would get better." She began removing the black wrapper from around her head. "Bisa said you opened the door. Why, Ezomo?"

Ezomo told his mother why. And when he finished, Yatta's eyes strayed out of the hut and stood outside watching the sky. She said nothing for a while, then called her gaze back inside to look at Ezomo. "And you did all that to save me?"

Ezomo nodded.

"Thank you, Ezomo." She hesitated. Words swayed on her tongue. "But it's not your job to save me. A lamb can't carry a sheep." She smiled. "If you want to help me, start contributing. Start helping your village." She drew a long breath. "Maybe one day your village will help you too." Her hand slipped underneath the blanket and retrieved a rag. Tucked inside of it was the golden leaf.

Ezomo's mouth fell open. "You didn't swallow it?"

"No," Yatta said, giving the leaf to Ezomo.

"Why not?"

"Steew! You expect me to swallow a strange leaf from a strange tree?"

"Then how are you still alive?"

"When Bisa told me about you opening the door, about how brave you had been, I knew I wanted to see the brave boy Bisa spoke about. I wanted to see my son."

Ezomo saw that his mother's eyes were filled with pride. He smiled. And then his smile faded. "I wish Papa was here to see me."

"Me too Ezomo."

"I hope he never forgets me."

Yatta took Ezomo's hand. "I'm certain he won't."

10

Help Arrives

The subject of every conversation in Sesa was Ezomo. Some said he had gone back to the evil village to gather more leaves. Others said a witch had helped him escape from the Valley, and he was now living in the swamp behind the door. A few said they had seen him near his hut, but that was impossible because he was banned from the village. The villagers talked and speculated and talked some more. Fire pits were lit. Songs were sung. Sesa was alive with stories.

When the evening left to go rest, the night arrived, bringing with it the hoots of owls and the chirps of grasshoppers. It was then that Oma pointed out that the moon had vanished from the sky. Some said that maybe the children were right, and the leopard had captured the moon.

Others said the moon was old and forgetful—it had simply departed too early. But it was Bisa who knew the truth. The moon hadn't been captured and it wasn't forgetful. Rather, it was hanging over the Valley and had arrived there when the hunters took Ezomo back to the forsaken place. And so that night, the Elders ordered Bisa to tell Ezomo to send the moon back to the sky where it belonged.

Bisa whizzed down into the Valley and relayed the message to Ezomo, Muja, and Chimama. "They say e better send the moon back to the sky or else. . . ."

Ezomo glanced at the moon hovering over the gorge. It was bright and full. "Tell them we don't know why the moon is here!"

"And why is it turning yellow?" Bisa remarked.

Ezomo watched as the moon turned from silver to yellow and then orange. Its big splotches separating into tiny spots.

"And why does it look like a leopard?" asked Bisa.

It was at that moment that Ezomo accepted a truth he wished was a lie. "I think the leopard led us to the village door on purpose that day in the forest. I think the leopard wanted us to find Ekewe. I think it intended to visit me on the anniversary of my father's death. It wanted me to know the truth."

"So the leopard is good?" Chimama asked.

"If not for the leopard, we would have never made it out of the swamp. We would not have known the truth about our parents or the crops. That leopard is good," Muja said.

But the leopard had also killed Ezomo's father, and this knowing tugged on Ezomo's heart. He inhaled the cold Valley air and allowed a restless thing in him to settle. He then turned and whispered something in Muja's ear, and Muja whispered it to Chimama, and Chimama whispered it to Ada, and Ada whispered it to Ofasa. Ofasa giggled.

"Tell them the leopard *is* keeping the moon here!" Ezomo said to Bisa.

Bisa looked suspicious. "How so? Why? Who?"

"If they let us go home," Ezomo continued, "we'll tell the leopard to let the moon go."

Bisa flapped his wings and flew away.

When Bisa told the Elders of Ezomo's demand, they fussed and fumed and refused to free Ezomo, Chimama, and Muja. And so the next day, the moon remained over the Valley and did not travel to Sesa. And still, the Elders remained stubborn. On the third day, however, the Elders visited the Valley, their faces troubled, their eyes red from lack of sleep.

"They say they will set one child free and see what happens," Bisa said. "They say they will send a rope down for the youngest."

"That's me." Ofasa giggled.

And so one end of a long rope was tossed into the Valley and tied around Ofasa's waist, and as soon as the boy was out, the moon inched away from the Valley.

"It worked!" Bisa shouted.

"Get them out!" Sao ordered.

They pulled Ada out and watched the moon inch even farther in the direction of the village. Next they pulled Chimama out and then Muja. And finally, Ezomo. By this time, news had traveled that the moon was almost back in Sesa.

"Take them out, too," Ezomo ordered, pointing to the forsaken people in the Valley.

And so, one by one, all the people sent to the Valley were released and set free. And the moon, grand and glorious, and wondrous and warm, began to shrink, its full body thinning and waning, its yellow face turning chalky and milky. They say on that night, the moon carried a tale, a long one streaming down like strips of sunlight, shimmering and shining, and sprinkling sun dust on every villager in Sesa.

"The leopard told me to tell you something," Ezomo said to the Elders when he was finally hoisted out of the gorge. "If you ever send anyone else to the Valley, it will come back and take the moon."

The Elders nodded solemnly although Sao, his face lined with vexation, glared at Ezomo and grumbled under his breath.

"Are we free to go now?" asked Chimama.

The Elders moved out of the way and let Ezomo, Muja, and Chimama go wherever they wished to go.

11

The Very End

The next day, Ezomo sat with his back resting against the trunk of the mango tree, watching Oma show the children how to tie a three-way knot. To his right was Chimama. Beside her sat Ada carrying Humongous on her shoulder. Muja and Ofasa sat on his left. The five of them were not allowed to sit anywhere else, for they had all done a terrible thing. So they sat together in the very back, under the shadows of the branches, under sunlight shining between leaves, whispering and giggling when Oma wasn't looking.

Bisa perched in a nearby tree, weaving the golden leaf into his nest and watching the children. He wished he had a better tale to carry. He wished he could say that the children were allowed to sit where they wanted, and that Toba was talking and Chima cooking. And that Yatta was completely well. But that wouldn't be the true story. Ezomo, Muja, and Chimama took a long journey to reach the same place. But they accepted the same place with a new understanding. They found happiness in sorrow and friendship in isolation. And though they had lost much, they had also gained plenty. Bisa knew that the fisherman doesn't always catch a fish and that the farmer doesn't always have a good harvest—but he also knows that they never go home empty-handed, and neither will the children.